PRAISE FOR WINTERKILL

'A sinister "twisted tragedy"' *The Times*

'Jónasson's Dark Iceland novels are instant classics and *Winterkill* is no exception – highly recommended' William Ryan

'The engaging Ari Thór returns in this darkly claustrophobic tale. Perfect mid-winter reading' Ann Cleeves

'Jónasson is an automatic must-read for me ... possibly the best Scandi writer working today' Lee Child

'*Winterkill* is a stunningly atmospheric story. Ari Thór Arason returns in this pitch-perfect, beautifully paced crime novel set in the blizzards of Icelandic springtime. Chilling and addictive. Ragnar Jónasson is at the top of his game. A master of the genre' Will Dean

'A perfect goodbye to a gritty and superb thriller series. Ari Thór is a memorable detective who will go down as one of the greats. I've loved all six books and the Dark Iceland series is one I shall return to again and again' Michael Wood

'Jónasson's punchy, straightforward prose is engrossing, and if the book's final revelations aren't necessarily surprising, they're eminently logical and satisfying. For those hankering for hearty storytelling in an unusual setting, *Winterkill* is a diverting mystery' *Foreword Reviews*

'Jónasson elegantly arranges things to make it appear as though no crime has taken place ... Yet when the finger of suspicion has no one to point at the effect is that everyone falls under consideration ... It's always the quiet places that you have to keep an eye on' *Strong Words*

'Ragnar Jónasson has always been an economical writer. His ability to convey complex emotions and situations in clear, concise language is a true gift' Bolo Books

'Emotional, atmospheric and deeply unsettling ... a series that has held me captivated from the opening lines of *Snowblind*' Bibliophile Book Club

'Anyone who loves classic crime fiction, slow-burning mysteries and police procedurals simply must check out Ragnar Jónasson's Dark Iceland books ... a wintry atmosphere, a chilling mystery, and a return for some of his iconic characters' Crime by the Book

'Top-class thriller writing. Good characters, good plot, very atmospheric – certainly recommended'
Independent Book Reviews

'Ragnar Jónasson is one of the best crime writers out there at the moment ... The atmospheric setting chilled me to the bone and that was even before some rather shocking twists were revealed, sending shivers down my spine!' My Chestnut Reading Tree

'A Ragnar Jónasson book has multiple characters, but for me, the one that always stands out is Iceland. The coldness really does seep off the pages' Swirl & Thread

'Gripping, claustrophobic, creepy (some of the characters were a bit sinister, like the father and son hiding out on an island), and clever' Rambling Mads

'Absolutely stunning ... The suspense-filled chapters quickly evolved into a fatal mystery where you suspect EVERYONE'
The Reading Closet

'A beautifully constructed novel with sparse, tight prose and great plotting. Jónasson is the absolute master of this genre, every word is carefully placed to intrigue, distract or entice'
Beverley Has Read

'Jónasson has become such a master ... The plotting is tightly constructed and the interweaving of threads feels so natural that the simple pleasure of its reading belies the complexity of its creation' Live Many Lives

'Jónasson's description is incredibly detailed and I was immediately transported to the locations in the novel' Portable Magic

'I'm a huge fan of Jónasson's books and his wonderfully sparse style. There's barely an ounce of fat on this tale, and it's just a joy to read, although over all too soon' Espresso Coco

'This is not a simple whodunnit. With a couple of almighty twists, Jónasson confounds our expectations ... the encore that the public demanded. Jónasson promises, and delivers, a storm worthy of the name' Café Thinking

'Taut, tenacious storytelling squeezes thoughts and feelings in this chilling read ... a stimulating and readable series' LoveReading

'A well-written murder mystery thriller, that will blow you away with its hard-hitting storyline' Surjit's Books Blog

'This is a masterclass in how to plot a crime story, with different threads interweaving and apparently innocuous details becoming significant. Nordic Noir at its best' Books, Life & Everything

'A masterpiece of understated, stark and terrifying storytelling, by the master of Icelandic crime writing. A true classic ... an utter triumph' Books Are My Cwtches

'Tightly written, well paced, extremely fine prose' The Literary Shed

'Impossible to tell which way it was going. I found myself constantly changing my mind about what was going to happen ... right until the end' Over-the-Rainbow Book Blog

'Jónasson expertly leads us along until a real shocker comes barrelling in and, in *Winterkill*, it's a shocker that will stay with you' Mumbling about...

PRAISE FOR RAGNAR JÓNASSON

'Chilling, creepy, perceptive, almost unbearably tense' Ian Rankin

'This is such a tense, gripping read' Anthony Horowitz

'Is this the best crime writer in the world today? ... Truly a master of his genre' *The Times*

'A world-class crime writer' *Sunday Times*

'This is Icelandic Noir of the highest order' *Daily Mail*

'Fans of dark crime fiction that doesn't pull punches will be amply rewarded' *Publishers Weekly*

'A vivid cast of characters, whose fears, ambitions, rivalries and longings are movingly universal' *Oprah Magazine*

'Traditional and beautifully finessed' *Independent*

'A distinctive blend of Nordic Noir and Golden Age detective fiction' *Guardian*

'Jónasson's true gift is for describing the daunting beauty of the fierce setting, lashed by blinding snowstorms that smother the village in "a thick, white darkness" that is strangely comforting' *New York Times*

'A chiller of a thriller' *Washington Post*

'The best sort of gloomy storytelling' *Chicago Tribune*

'The prose is stark and minimal, the mood dank and frost-tipped. It's also bleakly brilliant' *Metro*

'Jónasson's books have breathed new life into Nordic Noir' *Express*

'Required reading' *New York Post*

'Ragnar Jónasson writes with a chilling, poetic beauty' Peter James

'A truly chilling debut, perfect for fans of Karin Fossum and Henning Mankell' Eva Dolan

'An isolated community, subtle clueing, clever misdirection and more than a few surprises combine to give a modern-day Golden Age whodunnit' Dr John Curran

'A chilling, thrilling slice of Icelandic Noir' Thomas Enger

'A brilliantly crafted crime story that gradually unravels old secrets in a small Icelandic town … a talented Icelandic author. I can't wait to read more' Sarah Ward

'Puts a lively, sophisticated spin on the Agatha Christie model, taking it down intriguing dark alleys' *Kirkus Reviews*

Other books in the Dark Iceland Series

ABOUT THE AUTHOR

Ragnar Jónasson is author of the international bestselling Dark Iceland series, which has sold over 1.5 million books worldwide and is published in over thirty countries. His debut, *Snowblind,* went to number one in the kindle charts shortly after publication, and *Nightblind* (which also won the Mörda Dead Good Reader Award at Harrogate), *Blackout, Rupture* and *Whiteout* soon followed suit, hitting the number one spot around the world.

Ragnar was born in Reykjavík, Iceland, where he continues to work as a lawyer, and is co-founder of the Reykjavík international crime-writing festival, Iceland Noir. From the age of seventeen, Ragnar translated fourteen Agatha Christie novels into Icelandic. He has appeared on festival panels worldwide, and still lives in Reykjavík, with his wife and young daughters. Visit him on Twitter and Instagram @ragnarjo or at ragnarjonasson.com

ABOUT THE TRANSLATOR

David Warriner grew up in deepest Yorkshire, has lived in France and Quebec, and now calls British Columbia home. He translated Johana Gustawsson's *Blood Song* for Orenda Books (longlisted for the 2020 CWA Crime Fiction in Translation Dagger), and his translation of Roxanne Bouchard's *We Were the Salt of the Sea* was runner-up for the 2019 Scott Moncrieff Prize for French-English translation. Follow David on Twitter @givemeawave and on his website: wtranslation.ca.

Winterkill

Orenda Books
16 Carson Road
West Dulwich
London SE21 8HU
www.orendabooks.co.uk

This edition published by Orenda Books, 2020
First published in French as Sigló, 2020
Copyright © Ragnar Jónasson, 2020
English language translation copyright © David Warriner, 2020

A catalogue record for this book is available from the British Library.

Goldsboro Books signed hardback ISBN 978-1-913193-47-8
Hardback ISBN 978-1-913193-46-1
B-format paperback ISBN 978-1-913193-44-7
eISBN 978-1-913193-45-4

Printed and bound by CPI Group (UK) Ltd, Croydon CR0 4YY

For sales and distribution please contact info@orendabooks.co.uk

Ragnar Jónasson

Winterkill

Translated from the French edition
by David Warriner

ORENDA
BOOKS

*To all the friends of Ari Thór who asked me
to write one more book about him*

'Then all the ills of winter are swept away.'

Þ. Ragnar Jónasson (1913–2003)
Stories from Siglufjörður, 1997 (Trns. Quentin Bates)

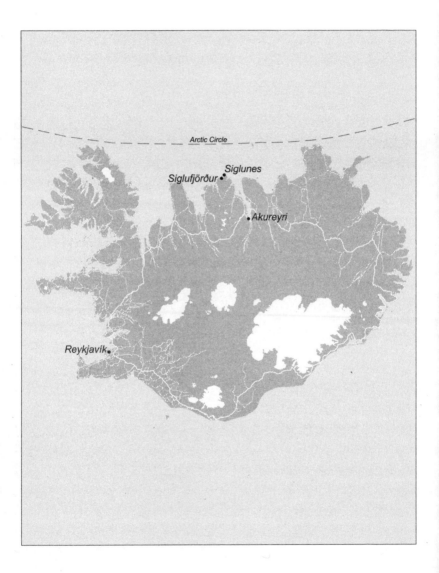

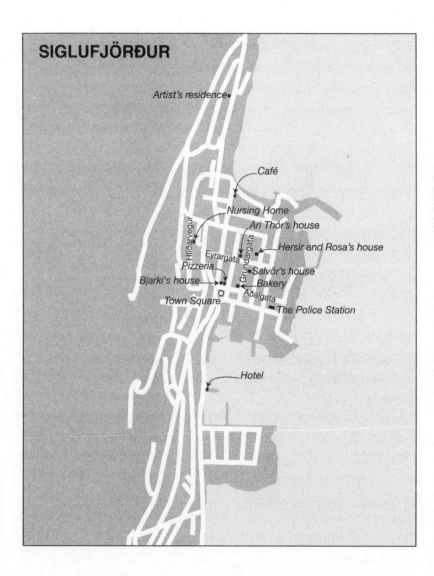

SIGLUFJÖRÐUR

Artist's residence

Café

Nursing Home

Ari Thór's house

Hlíðarvegur

Hersir and Rosa's house

Eyrargata

Grundargata

Pizzeria

Salvör's house

Bjarki's house

Bakery

Town Square

Aðalgata

The Police Station

Hotel

Pronunciation guide

Icelandic has a couple of letters that don't exist in other European languages and which are not always easy to replicate. The letter ð is generally replaced with a *d* in English, but we have decided to use the Icelandic letter to remain closer to the original names. Its sound is closest to the voiced *th* in English, as found in *th*en and ba*th*e.

The Icelandic letter þ is reproduced as *th*, as in *Th*orleifur, and is equivalent to an unvoiced *th* in English, as in *th*ing or *th*ump.

The letter *r* is generally rolled hard with the tongue against the roof of the mouth.

In pronouncing Icelandic personal and place names, the emphasis is always placed on the first syllable.

Ari Thór – AH-ree THOE-wr
Baldvina – BALD-veena
Bjarki – BYAHR-kee
Bolli – BOD-lee
Dóra – DOE-ra
Eggert – EGG-gerrt
Gudjón – GVOOTH-yoen
Hávardur – HOW-varth-oor
Hersir – HAIR-seer
hnútar – HNOO-tar
Hrólfur – HROEL-voor
Jenný – YENN-nee
Jóhann – YOE-han
Jónína – OE-neena
Kristín – KRIS-teen

Ögmundur – UGG-moon-door
Rósa – ROE-ssa
Salvör – SAL-vur
Sara – SAH-ra
Selma – SELL-ma
sírópskökur – SEE-roeps-KUR-koor
Stefnir – STEB-neer
Svavar – SVAH-var
Thorleifur – THOR-lay-voor
Thormódur – THOR-moe-thoor
Tómas – TOE-mas
Ugla – OOG-la
Unnur – OON-noor
Víkingur – VEE-kingg-oor

HOLY THURSDAY

1

'Police, Inspector Ari Thór Arason speaking.'

The emergency operator cut to the chase: 'We've just received a call from Siglufjörður; are you the duty officer tonight?'

❅

Night and day were much the same in Siglufjörður in summer, when the sun barely set at all. It was Ari Thór's favourite time of year. It was just a couple of months away now, and for him, it couldn't come soon enough. He loved the sense of infinite freedom that came with the long hours of daylight in the north of Iceland.

It was a far cry from the darkness and snow that blanketed the town in winter.

Ari Thór was wide awake when the phone rang. He couldn't sleep, no matter how hard he tried. He was still using the master bedroom in his place on Eyrargata. The same room he had shared with Kristín and Stefnir before she and the little one moved to Sweden.

He had found it hard to adjust when he first moved there from Reykjavík, but the blizzards and gloomy days no longer brought on the same feeling of claustrophobia. He hardly ever felt homesick anymore. In recent years, Siglufjörður had experienced the ripple effects from the new wave of prosperity that was sweeping across southern Iceland in the wake of the financial crisis. Now, tourists from all over the world flocked to the small town every summer. Even in winter, people came to enjoy the local ski slopes, most of them from other places in Iceland. Easter had become an especially popular time for visitors, and now, on the eve of the long weekend, it looked like the slopes were going to be busy.

Ari Thór was in his thirties now, but he felt that his life was back at square one. He lived alone and he hardly saw his son anymore. He couldn't imagine being able to salvage what was left of his relationship with Kristín. They had exhausted all the options, so to speak.

Truth be told, he had settled into a comfortable routine and he was reluctant to do anything that might rock the boat. He had been promoted to inspector in Siglufjörður after years of aspiring to the role, so he was now in charge at the police station. At some point, he would have to decide whether he was happy with what he had achieved. He knew that it would be hard for him to go any further if he stayed in Siglufjörður, that was if he decided to keep climbing the rungs of the career ladder. It wasn't just that he had reached the most senior rank at the small-town police station; it was the fact that, even if he excelled in his current position, there were no higher-ups close by to see his good work.

Tómas, his old boss, had left Siglufjörður and moved south to take up a position in Reykjavík. For a while now, he had been encouraging Ari Thór to follow his example, saying Ari Thór should let Tómas know when he was ready to do the same, and he would put in a good word for him. Ari Thór wasn't sure the offer still stood, however, as it had been a long time since Tómas had mentioned it. And he was all too aware that Tómas wasn't getting any younger and must be close to retirement. Soon, Ari Thór would lose his only advocate at police headquarters in Reykjavík. Once that door closed, he might be stuck up north for good, whether he liked it or not.

Ari Thór's consternation about his future tended to prey on his mind in the dead of night, and now was no exception. When the sun came up, though, he always managed to clear his head, resolving to keep taking one day at a time. But he knew the clock was ticking. Soon, he would have to make up his mind. Maybe he would decide that he was right where he wanted to be, here in Siglufjörður. He still needed to give the matter some serious thought.

There would be no time to dwell on the question over the Easter weekend, however. He would be too busy doting on little Stefnir. Ari Thór's heart was already skipping a beat at the thought of seeing him again, even though it was just for a few days. His son had turned three at Christmas, but Ari Thór had missed out on all the celebrations.

Six months earlier, Kristín had made the decision to further her medical training by going to university in Sweden. Ari Thór didn't hold it against her. Iceland provided excellent training in general medicine, but like many doctors, she wanted to become a specialist, and the time had finally come for her to stop putting things off and pursue her ambition, and that meant studying abroad. As Kristín's plans became clear, she and Ari Thór had discussed Stefnir's future in light of the move. Kristín had suggested that she take the boy with her 'in the beginning'; they could think about other options down the line. She had promised to bring Stefnir back to Iceland at Christmas and at Easter, perhaps more often, and Ari Thór had been planning to take holiday time in the summer to see them in Sweden. He hadn't objected, despite the terrible sense of dread that filled him at the thought of seeing his son so rarely. He wanted to avoid any kind of conflict with Kristín.

Ari Thór tossed and turned in bed, trying to get comfortable. Curling up on his side, he took a deep breath and released it with a long sigh. He had to get some sleep. Tomorrow – no, today, he corrected himself – was Thursday, and his last day on duty before the long Easter weekend. Kristín and Stefnir would be arriving that evening.

It was nearly three in the morning. More than two hours since he had gone to bed, and he was still wide awake.

Eventually, he admitted defeat and got up.

Damn it. He couldn't afford a sleepless night, not now, when he was supposed to be ready to enjoy a weekend with his son. But anxiety only fuelled the fire of sleeplessness, and now he didn't even feel tired anymore.

There wasn't much furniture in the bedroom besides some shelves filled with old books that the former homeowners hadn't bothered to take with them. Ari Thór had sometimes leafed through the pages of these volumes, mostly when he was trying to sleep and needed some distraction from his thoughts. He plucked a book from the shelf, almost at random, and laid his head on the pillow again.

Try as he might, Ari Thór couldn't shake a niggling feeling of apprehension about the weekend ahead. For the first time, he was leaving the station in the hands of Ögmundur, a young recruit who had moved north for his first posting. What he lacked in experience, he more than made up for with his eagerness to learn.

Since Ari Thór had taken on the inspector's post, he had been forced to make do with temporary replacements and officers seconded from Ólafsfjörður or Akureyri – never the same person from one case to the next. But recently, he had received approval to hire an officer for a full-time position. There had been no shortage of interest in the job, and some of the applicants boasted a wealth of experience, but Ari Thór had chosen to hire this young man, who was fresh out of police training school.

In spite of their difference in character, Ari Thór saw something of his younger self in Ögmundur. He remembered how Tómas had shown him the ropes when he first came to Siglufjörður. Now the tables were turned, and Ari Thór was the experienced officer putting the young rookie through his paces. He had to admit, though, that he had struggled to build the rapport with Ögmundur that Tómas had built with him, in spite of there being a narrower age gap between them.

After trying to find sleep in the pages of a book for what seemed like an age, Ari Thór went down the rickety old stairs to the kitchen. There, he poured himself a glass of water and snacked on a piece of dried fish as he flicked through yesterday's newspaper. He shouldn't have bothered; there was nothing new in there, just the same rehashed stories. The only thing that really caught his eye was the weather forecast. It wasn't great. It looked like heavy storms were expected in the north right after the Easter weekend. That was the thing about winter up here; no sooner had you dug yourself out after one blizzard than you had to prepare for the next one.

He really couldn't afford a sleepless night; he wouldn't last the day.

Ari Thór was on call, but more often than not, the streets of the little town were deserted overnight and the police station was a haven of calm. Usually the only calls were complaints about drunks making too much noise on their way home.

Ari Thór had gone back to bed – but was still wide awake – when the phone rang.

'A passerby has found what seems to be the body of a young woman lying in the street. An ambulance is on the way, just in case,' the operator at the emergency call centre said in a neutral tone.

Ari Thór hurriedly pulled his uniform on, pinning the phone to his ear with his shoulder.

'Where?'

'On the main street, Aðalgata.'

'Who made the call?'

'The man's name is Gudjón Helgason. He said he would stay on the scene until the police arrived.'

The name didn't sound familiar.

Two minutes later, Ari Thór was fully dressed and stepping outside into the night. He lived just around the corner from the main street, so it would only take a moment for him to get there on foot. It was a frigid, windless night and the stars were sparkling in the sky. Nature up here was always wild and unbridled, but at this time of year, there was something not just darker about it, but somehow deeper and more distant.

Ari Thór arrived on the scene at the same time as the ambulance. As he turned onto Aðalgata, a shiver ran down his spine.

On the edge of the pavement, a young woman was lying in a pool of her own blood, her body twisted into so unnatural a position, there was little doubt that she must have plunged from a great height. It didn't take a doctor to figure out that she was dead. It looked like all the blood had come from her head; her skull was likely fractured.

As Ari Thór approached the body, he realised the woman was probably even younger than he had first thought –

possibly still in her teens. He drew in a sharp breath as he saw her face.

Oh, hell.

Her gaze was eerily absent, her eyes wide open but empty, as if staring into nothing.

Ari Thór immediately knew it was a sight that would haunt him forever.

2

Ari Thór was no stranger to wandering the streets at night. It didn't matter if it was the height of summer or the dead of winter, there was something magical about the experience of going for a stroll when no one else was around. The town always seemed so peaceful under the blanket of nocturnal silence. For a brief moment, he had that familiar sense of floating in the peaceful calm, but the gravity of the situation returned and shattered the stillness.

The few people on the scene seemed to be awaiting his orders, all except the doctor from the hospital, who was already crouching beside the young woman's body. Other than the doctor, Ari Thór saw two paramedics, and, behind them, a man who looked to be in his thirties, wearing a down jacket and a woolly hat and sporting a full beard – presumably this was Gudjón, the man who had called the emergency services.

Ari Thór felt like he was frozen to the spot. Now more than ever, he was aware of the weight of the responsibility on his shoulders. Since he had been promoted to inspector, life in Siglufjörður had followed its usual uneventful course and, to his great relief, he hadn't had any major crimes to deal with. Days came and went with a comforting lack of excitement as the police were called to deal with nothing more serious than the occasional report of drug use, highway-code violations or night-time noise. But now this young woman had been found dead in the middle of the main street. Ari Thór looked at her again before lifting his gaze to take in the surroundings.

The lifeless body was lying on the pavement in front of a two-storey house with dormer windows in the roof, suggesting a third level of living space in the attic. It looked like there was a rooftop balcony as well. Ari Thór's first thought was that the young woman must have fallen from up there, as chilling as that prospect was.

The doctor stood up. Her name was Baldvina, and she had only been in Siglufjörður since the beginning of January. Doctors never stayed around here for very long. Turnover at the hospital had been high in recent years, with one doctor after another moving on to better things in bigger places as soon as an opportunity came along, or leaving to pursue further training, like Kristín had done. Baldvina was a little younger than Ari Thór. He had the sense that she was competent, based on the few times their paths had crossed.

'Well, she's certainly dead. Most likely as a result of her fall,' Baldvina said, turning to look up at the roof of the building, pre-empting Ari Thór's question. 'I suspect she fell from that balcony up there. But that's something for you to find out, of course. Is it all right for us to move the body?'

Ari Thór felt a knot in his stomach. This was the first violent death he would have to investigate as the officer in charge. He was anxious to do things properly.

'Yes, but just let me take a few photos first. And we'll also have to secure the scene for forensic examination.'

Ari Thór knew it would take a while for the forensics team to travel to Siglufjörður. But he couldn't bring himself to let the poor young woman wallow here in her own blood for longer than she had to. It was a matter of respect. He didn't want to leave her body exposed for all to see. This was the main shopping street in town, and the sun would soon be rising. He was also wary of any curious night-birds who might be attracted by all the unusual activity and swoop in for a closer look.

Ari Thór used his phone to take some photos of the scene. Then he called Ögmundur to let him know what had happened. 'I need you to come and join me on Aðalgata as quickly as you can.'

'Yes, er, of course,' his half-asleep junior officer replied after a brief moment of hesitation.

Ögmundur had shown himself to be positive by nature and seemed keen to embrace any challenge, though in all honesty his workload so far had not been particularly demanding. Not only had it been an uneventful winter, Ari Thór had also spared his new recruit some of the more mundane duties of the job, preferring to let him settle in at his own pace. Somehow, though, Ögmundur had already managed to make more friends in Siglufjörður than Ari Thór had in all the years he had lived here. The young rookie seemed to be very quick to earn people's trust – obviously a desirable quality in this job. It also turned out that Ögmundur had played for the Icelandic national football team – the junior team, in fact, but that made no difference to Ari Thór – and his enthusiasm for the sport, a popular topic of conversation around these parts, made it easy for him to engage with people.

Ari Thór explained the situation to Ögmundur on the other end of the line. 'She must have fallen from the rooftop balcony,' he added. 'We don't know yet if it was an accident or if it was, er … suicide. That's what we'll have to find out. And time is of the essence.'

On receiving Ari Thór's go-ahead, the paramedics lifted the lifeless body of the young woman onto a trolley and rolled it into the ambulance, leaving nothing but a gruesome red pool on the pavement, a chilling remnant of what had happened. Under the glow of a streetlight and amidst the shadows of the night, the blood looked almost too bright to be real. For a second Ari Thór thought the scene looked like a theatre set.

Now he turned to the man who had been standing in the background, barely moving a muscle, keeping his head down. 'Good evening. You must be Gudjón?'

The man nodded before murmuring a hesitant 'yes'.

'I'm Inspector Ari Thór Arason. Can you tell me what happened? Was it you who called the police?'

'Yes. Well, I called the emergency number, but I didn't really know what to say. I don't have a clue what happened.'

The words seemed to make him short of breath. He kept rubbing his beard as he spoke, and his eyes darted from side to side, without meeting Ari Thór's.

Ari Thór listened and waited. It was too soon to launch straight into another question. Experience had taught him that people who were nervous, as Gudjón seemed to be, tended to fill a silence.

'I just, well, found her like that, just lying there. At first I thought she had fallen. Slipped and fallen on the street, I mean. I went over and was about to help her get up when I noticed … when I realised she was dead. Then I called the emergency services – straight away.'

'Did you touch anything?' Ari Thór asked after a brief pause.

'I … I can't remember. Maybe I gave her a little shake to make sure, but it seemed so obvious that she was dead.'

Ari Thór nodded. 'Did you notice anyone else in the vicinity?'

'No, there was no one else around. Only me. It was quite a shock to see her lying there. Do you think she jumped?'

'It's hard to say right now,' Ari Thór replied, then pursued his line of questioning. 'It's four in the morning now, so you were out and about at around three-thirty, is that correct?'

'Yes, yes, that's right.'

'Why was that?'

'I was just out for a walk, that's all.'

'In the middle of the night?' Ari Thór raised an eyebrow.

'I find the cold invigorating. The skies are clear, and there's not a breath of wind, just the fresh sea air to fill your lungs. It's a joy to wander the streets in this weather.'

Ari Thór wasn't convinced, though, to be fair, he often went for a walk around town after dark, too – not that he was going to admit that to Gudjón. There was something about the silence that descended on these streets in the dead of night. That damned, elusive silence.

'Day and night?'

'I prefer to walk at night. It's quieter. More soothing for the soul.'

'Do you live in Siglufjörður, Gudjón?'

Gudjón hesitated.

'I do at the moment, yes. I'm here for three months, on an artist's retreat.'

'And where are you staying?'

'There's an artist's residence not far from here, on the waterfront, just on the edge of town.'

'And have you been here long?'

'Since January,' Gudjón replied. Now he seemed to be feeling the chill of the night. It looked like it was making him uncomfortable.

'I see,' Ari Thór said, marking a pause. 'What's your discipline?'

'What do you mean?'

'What's your artistic discipline? Painting, or music, for example.'

'Painting. Yes, painting. Well, I paint, and I draw. Perhaps you saw the posters for my exhibition the other day. Landscapes of Siglufjörður. They're all for sale.'

'No, I must have missed those. Do you know her?'

'Who?'

'The dead woman.'

Gudjón shivered. 'What? No, of course not. I have no idea who she is ... er, was. Why would I know her? I'm not from round here.'

'What makes you so sure she was a local?'

'I ... well, how am I to know? I don't know what you're insinuating. All I did was call the police. I've never seen that young woman before.'

'You have to admit, Gudjón, it's a bit strange to be wandering around in the middle of the night.'

'I'm an artist, for heaven's sake!' he protested, as if that word could justify all manner of quirks and sins. His breath was coming in fits and starts, and he was struggling to string his words together. 'Look, I walk the streets at night to find inspiration, then I go home and I draw. I sleep in the daytime. You're welcome to ... come over and look at my work if you like. That way you'll see I'm not lying to you.'

'That won't be necessary for now, but I'm sure I'll be in touch as the investigation progresses,' Ari Thór explained. 'However, I would ask that you come by the station later today so we can take a formal statement.'

Gudjón's reluctance was palpable. 'Is that really necessary? I've got nothing to hide, but to be perfectly honest, I have absolutely no desire to be grilled by the police any more than I have been already.' Still struggling to catch his breath, he added: 'The only … the only thing I did was my civic duty, when I picked up the phone to call you, all right?'

'Listen, a young woman – perhaps she was still just a teenager – is dead, and you discovered her body. We have to take your statement for the purposes of the investigation. We have no reason to assume that you might have somehow been involved in her death.' Ari Thór was reluctant to sugar-coat his words too much; he still wasn't entirely satisfied with Gudjón's explanation.

'Well, I certainly hope you're not going to accuse an innocent bystander of any wrongdoing!'

❄

Gudjón was still huffing and puffing when Ögmundur turned the corner onto Aðalgata, at the wheel of his little red Mazda, an older, sporty convertible that could still turn heads. A low-slung car like that wasn't the most practical in the snow, but after a few days of unseasonably mild temperatures and rain, the streets were clear that night. He parked across the street and ran over to Ari Thór and Gudjón.

'Sorry to keep you waiting, I came as quickly as I could. Do you think she jumped?'

His eyes darted down to the pool of blood, then up to the balcony on the roof.

'Thanks, I appreciate it,' Ari Thór said. 'This is Gudjón Helgason. He was out for a night-time stroll when he stumbled upon the body. I've asked him to come down to the station later. When he does, would you kindly take his statement, Ögmundur?'

'Of course, I'll take care of it.' Ögmundur smiled and

reached out to shake the man's hand. 'Hi, Gudjón. Nice to meet you. My name's Ögmundur. I'm a police officer here.'

'That will be all for now. You're free to go on your way. Thank you for your cooperation.' Ari Thór dismissed Gudjón with a curt nod.

Ögmundur's informal tone when speaking to members of the public was something that got on Ari Thór's nerves, though he had to admit it often helped to loosen their tongues.

'Enjoy the rest of your walk,' he added, through gritted teeth.

Hauled out of bed in the middle of the night when he was already deprived of sleep, Ari Thór was struggling to put on as cheerful a face as the young rookie.

3

'Stay out here,' said Ari Thór. 'I want you to call forensics. And keep an eye on the scene until they get here, OK?'

Ögmundur nodded indifferently. 'If you insist, but I don't really see the point, Ari Thór. You can see for yourself, there's nothing but blood on the ground. I'd be better going inside the building to make sure no one goes out onto the balcony.'

Ari Thór stuck to his guns. 'Just keep an eye on the entrance, all right? I'll go inside and take a look around the building.'

The front door was locked. Judging by the number of doorbells, the old house had been converted into two flats – one on each floor.

Ögmundur peered over Ari Thór's shoulder. 'Do you know the people who live here?'

'No,' Ari Thór said, shaking his head. The labels on the doorbells indicated only that the occupants of the ground-floor flat were named Jónína and Jóhann, and that a man by the name of Bjarki lived upstairs.

Ari Thór tried the bell for the downstairs flat. He didn't have to wait long before the door clicked open. In a doorway at the foot of the stairs stood an elderly man in pyjamas, who seemed wide awake.

'My wife and I were waiting for you. We've been watching what was going on out there,' the man said with a quiver of hesitation.

Evidently, they must have been standing in the dark, because Ari Thór hadn't noticed any light in the windows.

'So, what happened? Who was that, lying in the street? Are they dead?'

'Can I come in for a moment?'

'Oh yes, of course,' the man replied, extending a limp, clammy hand. 'I'm Jóhann.'

Ari Thór had a sense of foreboding. Something didn't seem right here. He followed the man into the gloomy flat and, in the living room, saw the shadow of a woman sitting on a sofa, beside a window that looked out onto the street. Presumably, this was Jónína. She didn't say a word as he approached.

Ari Thór took the lead. 'I'm sorry to disturb you. A young woman died here tonight. Did you happen to notice anything?'

'Nothing at all,' Jóhann replied decisively. 'Who was it?'

'I don't know yet. Perhaps you have an idea? Is there a young woman or a teenage girl who lives in the building?'

'No, no, just Bjarki upstairs, but ... sometimes he rents the flat out to strangers on Airy ... oh, heavens, Jónína, what's it called again?'

His wife remained tight-lipped. They both looked to be well north of seventy. Ari Thór wished he could pick Tómas's brain. His old boss had known just about everyone in town – where they worked and who was related to whom.

'Is he at home at the moment, do you think?'

The couple exchanged a glance.

'I don't think so,' Jóhann replied. 'He's always coming and going. He spends a lot of time in Reykjavík. But he's originally from here. I haven't seen him for a day or two.'

Jónína finally opened her mouth. 'No, he's not at home.' Her words were quiet but were said with conviction. 'I would have run into him, or at least heard if he was here.'

'You can't see everything, darling. We can't know all the comings and goings in the building, can we?'

His words seemed stilted, as if he were trying to send his wife a message. Ari Thór looked out the window and realised that anyone standing there probably wouldn't be able to see who was ringing the doorbell.

'When you said he was from here, did you mean him, or his family?' he asked.

'Him. He's a Siglufjörður boy,' Jónína replied. 'I remember his father. Bjarki was born here, then the family moved away, like so many others. Once the herring had all gone, there wasn't much to do around here.'

'Now, people are coming back and it's bringing life to the town again,' Jóhann added.

'We never left, of course,' said Jónína, folding her arms across her chest with a frown, as if to signal the end of the conversation.

'How do you get up to the balcony?' Ari Thór asked.

'The balcony? Why do you want to know that?' Jóhann seemed to have forgotten why the police were there. Then: 'Oh, yes, of course. Let me show you the way. There's a door off the attic, up in the eaves. In the old days, that space saw more use than it does now. Bjarki's grandparents used to live in this house. Then it was converted into flats and we bought the place on the ground floor. We were wanting to downsize, you see. Before we moved in here we had a detached house a bit further out of town, but it was so much work to keep it looking nice. Anyway, they made the attic into a common space for both flats, more of a place to store things than to spend any time. It's too cold up there to sit around. And we never go out onto that balcony. Jónína has no end of trouble getting up the stairs. And I doubt Bjarki spends much time out there either. He's always got his nose buried in his books. A fine young man, he is,' Jóhann added with a smile.

Again, Ari Thór had the feeling that something wasn't right about the way the man was talking. It seemed to him that Jóhann was nervous, and was trying to hide the fact by being overly chatty.

Jóhann led the way back to the entrance of the building and motioned for Ari Thór to follow him as he started up the stairs at a snail's pace. There was a certain old-fashioned charm about the creaky staircase. The time-worn wooden treads were a slightly lighter shade than the handrail, which seemed to have fared better over the years. The walls were decorated with pale-blue wallpaper.

When Jóhann reached the landing, he took a moment to catch his breath and pointed to a door.

'That's where the historian lives.'

'Bjarki? He's a historian?' Ari Thór asked.

'He's doing some research for the town council about people from Siglufjörður who emigrated to North America. The council must have a bit of money to play with if they can fund a project like that. The economy must be doing all right at the moment, I suppose, with all the road work, tourists and whatnot,' Jóhann mumbled, trying to gather the strength to tackle the next flight of stairs.

'I didn't know people from around here were part of that wave of emigration,' Ari Thór admitted.

'Apparently about fifteen thousand Icelanders from all over the country went over there around the turn of the century, and a fair few people from here ended up in Canada – in the province of Manitoba, I think Bjarki said. I'm not exactly a bookworm, but it's still an interesting research topic, don't you think? Right, off we go.'

They continued up the next flight of stairs, which ended abruptly at a closed door, with no landing.

'Here, let me open it,' said Ari Thór, keen to prevent someone who wasn't wearing gloves inadvertently messing up any fingerprints that might be on the door handle. 'It isn't locked, is it?'

'No, it never is.'

Ari Thór gently pushed the door open and tiptoed carefully into the attic room. At first glance, nothing seemed to be particularly out of place. The temperature up here was freezing, though, and Ari Thór soon saw why: the door leading to the balcony was ajar.

'Wait here, Jóhann, and don't touch anything,' he said with authority.

Ari Thór inspected the attic room without seeing anything suspicious. There were no signs of a struggle, but the door left ajar suggested that someone had been there recently. Cautiously, he stepped out into the early morning and drew a deep breath of icy, salty air. The view from the rooftop was certainly impressive. Ari Thór couldn't help but gaze in wonder at the panorama of mountains, which framed the town and fjord at his feet.

There was nothing immediately suspicious on the balcony either. The previous few days of rain and unseasonably mild temperatures had melted the snow that would normally have accumulated, so there were no footprints to confirm that the young woman had been there.

Ari Thór went back inside and found Jóhann at the top of the stairs, where he had left him. 'This room will have to be sealed off,' he said. 'The officer downstairs will take care of it. Don't let anyone else inside the building, all right?'

The elderly man nodded.

'Is there a back door to the building?' Ari Thór asked.

'Yes,' Jóhann admitted, looking more and more

uncomfortable. 'Well, it leads into Bjarki's flat. It's probably locked.'

'But you can't get out to the balcony from there, can you?'

'No, not unless … not unless you were to go through his flat and come this way, of course.'

'Excuse me,' said an impatient Ari Thór, hurrying past Jóhann and down the stairs to the landing below. He knocked on Bjarki's door.

There was no answer.

'I don't think he's at home,' Jóhann said.

Ari Thór accompanied the man downstairs without another word.

Jónína was standing in the doorway waiting for them.

'I'm going to leave you both in peace now,' Ari Thór said. 'With a bit of luck, you'll manage to get back to sleep.'

A thought occurred to him just as he was stepping outside. 'The front door was locked when we got here. Is that always the case?'

'These days, yes. It never used to be, though, in the old days.'

'So, if she … if the young woman was able to access the balcony, she must have had a key to the building.'

This time, as the elderly couple exchanged another glance, Ari Thór knew for sure that they were hiding something. He waited and let the silence do his job for him.

'Well, someone did come to the door tonight,' Jóhann stammered reluctantly.

'I see,' Ari Thór said gently.

'Someone rang the intercom and it woke us up. It happens sometimes, with different people staying there. Jónína, my wife … she buzzed them in.'

'Is that true?' Ari Thór turned to the elderly woman.

'Yes,' she sighed, barely loud enough for him to hear. 'Obviously I had no idea things would come to this...'

'Were you able to see who was at the door?'

They exchanged another glance, then Jóhann shook his head. 'No, but it must have been the girl who jumped, don't you think?'

'There's no one staying in the flat upstairs at the moment, not that we know of, but we can't always tell...' Jónína added. 'Plus, whoever rang the doorbell might have come in and gone right back out again, or not even come inside at all.'

'That's right,' Jóhann sputtered. 'And I hope ... Listen, my poor Jónína has been beside herself since the ambulance came. Neither of us could get back to sleep after the doorbell rang.'

'How long was it between then and the time the ambulance arrived?'

'Three quarters of an hour, perhaps a bit longer.'

Ari Thór frowned. Everything seemed to suggest that the young woman had entered the building in order to jump from the rooftop. But he couldn't determine that with any degree of certainty, because he didn't know how long she had been lying in the street before Gudjón happened upon the scene.

'Thank you,' Ari Thór said, through gritted teeth. 'You should have told me that straight away.'

'I know we should have, but my wife was in shock,' Jóhann replied, as if that were an excuse. 'We didn't set out to hide anything from you at all, we were just waiting for the right time to tell you.'

'I see. Please keep it to yourselves, in any case. The last thing we need is for rumours to get around.' He looked Jóhann, then Jónína, in the eye.

'Yes, of course. We'll be careful,' the elderly man replied.

'You don't think … that it's my fault, do you?' his wife asked, her downcast eyes filling with sorrow and guilt.

If the woman had been planning to kill herself, Ari Thór thought, she would have found a way to do it whether she managed to gain access to the balcony or not. There was always a way. But he had long since abandoned any inclination to rub ointment on bruised souls. His theology studies were but a distant memory now. Only a handful of stubborn locals persisted in referring to him as 'The Reverend' – a moniker he had reluctantly earned that first winter in Siglufjörður.

Ari Thór tended to take a less philosophical approach to his work these days. His job was to uphold the law and ensure order in the town. And to try and figure out why a young woman had decided to end her life in such an abrupt way – if this was indeed a suicide.

It was not his prerogative to give this old woman absolution.

'Was it your fault? That's hard to say,' he replied coldly. 'The investigation is only just beginning.'

4

'Oh, dear me, Ari Thór, I don't think I'll ever get used to hearing news like this, will I?'

The Reverend Eggert hadn't changed a bit in the seven years Ari Thór had spent in Siglufjörður. He was a man of indeterminate age, with soft words and even temper who was likely to carry his pastoral vocation well into retirement. He filled his free time with writing and seemed to lead a quiet, happy life in the small town. Ari Thór had always been impressed by the genuine interest this man of the Church took in his fellow citizens, and this was one of the reasons why he had asked him for help in identifying the young woman who had died. Even if it meant rousing him in the middle of the night.

'Her name is … was Unnur,' Reverend Eggert said. 'She was confirmed right here in my church, the poor child. What a terrible thing to happen to her. Such a charming girl, she was. Cheerful, well-mannered and committed to her studies. You know, Ari Thór, I really am surprised that this has happened to her, of all people. There are youngsters in town who are struggling, who have found themselves mixed up in drugs and whatnot, and I could quite easily see them meeting a tragic end like this, but not Unnur. I … I…'

'You can't believe it?'

'No. I don't think she could ever have brought herself to do such a thing.'

❋

Now, the two of them were standing outside the house where Unnur's mother lived. Ari Thór was dreading the moment that would come when the door opened. This wasn't the first time he had been the bearer of unbearable news. And he needed no reminding of the day when the police had knocked at the door to announce that his mother had died in a tragic accident. He had been just thirteen years old, but the memory was all too fresh in his mind. He remembered every detail of that fateful moment: the sound of the rain streaming down outside, the smell in the air, even the words the police officers had said.

These things would likely continue to haunt Unnur's mother too. In years to come, she would think back to this moment and see the cloudless sky of the breaking dawn. She would smell the salty tang of the still, cold air. And sense the impending threat of the snow looming just beyond the horizon.

Unnur's mother lived in a big old house on Grundargata, just around the corner from where her daughter's body had been found. All of the windows were dark. There was an air of serenity about the place, a calm that would soon be shattered.

Ari Thór pressed the doorbell and waited, casting a glance at the man by his side. Reverend Eggert placed a cautious hand on Ari Thór's shoulder.

'Why don't you let me do the talking, my friend?'

It was a while before a light snapped on inside and someone came downstairs. The woman who opened the door looked to be somewhere north of forty. Her pyjamas, tousled hair and bleary eyes suggested she had been fast asleep until a moment ago.

An expression of surprise and concern cracked her face as she recognised the reverend and saw Ari Thór's uniform.

'Salvör?' Ari Thór asked.

'Yes. What … what's wrong?' she stammered. 'Has something happened?'

'We need to talk to you. It's about your daughter,' Reverend Eggert said. 'Can we come in?'

Salvör stepped aside to let them into the house and closed the door behind them. She turned the light on in the living room and seemed to freeze. She didn't think to invite the visitors to sit down, and they didn't ask.

'Unnur is here.' Salvör spoke the words with confidence. 'She's in her room, sleeping.'

For a second, Ari Thór doubted his certainty. Maybe the reverend had been mistaken. Maybe the young woman whose body they had found in the street was someone else's daughter. He found himself secretly crossing his fingers, hoping to delay the inevitable.

Beside him, the Reverend Eggert paused in stillness for a moment. As if the shadow of a doubt had crossed his mind, too.

'Perhaps I should come with you and check,' he wisely suggested.

Salvör led the way and the reverend followed her down the hall. Ari Thór waited in the living room, still holding on to a glimmer of hope, though he knew it would be in vain.

When they returned, the look on the mother's face left no doubt. They had been gone for a long while, so Reverend Eggert must have tactfully chosen to break the news to her in private. Ari Thór appreciated the gesture. Salvör was crying. The tears were streaming down her cheeks.

'My dear Ari Thór, I think I'm going to stay for a while,' the reverend said gravely. 'Do you have any pressing questions for Salvör? Anything that can't wait?'

Ari Thór hesitated. All his questions could obviously wait, but he was conscious of his responsibilities and had to make sure he didn't let his emotions cloud his judgement.

'Please accept my sincerest condolences, Salvör,' he said. 'We'll talk another time, if necessary. For now, I just have one question for you. Was there anything about your daughter's behaviour recently that might suggest she ... had been thinking about...'

'...Taking her life?' the reverend ventured.

Salvör shook her head vehemently. 'No, no, no! Absolutely not. Not an inkling,' she sobbed. 'She was a bubbly teenage girl with her whole life ahead of her...'

Ari Thór knew appearances could be deceptive. Depression often lurked unseen beneath the surface. Still, it wasn't the answer he had expected to hear. Everything seemed to suggest that Unnur had thrown herself off the balcony. Everything pointed to a simple conclusion: that she had set out to end her own life. But judging by her mother's insistence to the contrary, this unfortunate matter would call for further investigation.

Ari Thór said his goodbyes and disappeared into the remaining shadows of the night.

5

It was past noon when Kristín called. Ari Thór hadn't expected to hear from her so soon. She and little Stefnir were supposed to be taking the afternoon flight to Akureyri before driving the remaining short distance to Siglufjörður.

'Hi, Ari.'

She was still the only one who just called him 'Ari'. The warmth in her voice reminded him of happier times, before either of them had even thought about doing anything that might throw their relationship into jeopardy. Part of him wanted to lay all the blame at her feet, but in truth they had both been at fault. The sound of her voice gave him butterflies in his stomach. There was obviously still a spark between the two of them. But Ari Thór didn't plan to put any more work into rekindling things.

'Oh hi! You must be taking off soon, I imagine?'

'Believe it or not, the plane's already landed and I'm on the road to Siglufjörður. Well, we both are, I mean.'

'Already?'

'Yes, we managed to catch an earlier flight. Listen, there's been a change of plans. The holiday replacement shifts I was supposed to be working at the hospital in Akureyri have been cancelled, so I can enjoy some proper time off at Easter at last.'

'Fantastic! Are you still going to stay at your friend's place in Akureyri, then, once you've dropped Stefnir here with me?'

Kristín paused for a moment before she answered.

'Actually, I thought I might stay in Siglufjörður, with the two of you ... if that's all right. I know it's still your weekend to have him, but I'd love to celebrate Easter with Stefnir too, if I can.'

'Yes, of course,' Ari Thór replied.

He was proud of how well they had managed their breakup. There had been no big arguments and no need to resort to mediation. That said, he was still struggling to come to terms with the fact that, this past Christmas, she had told him that she and Stefnir weren't coming back to Siglufjörður for the holidays – despite what they had agreed – and had made it clear that he wasn't welcome to visit them in Sweden either, saying she wanted to give Stefnir the chance to get used to their new arrangement without there being any drama.

'Just come and stay here,' he found himself saying, without really stopping to think about whether or not that was a good idea.

'Er … I've already booked a hotel room,' Kristín hastily replied. 'Maybe we can take turns to look after Stefnir this weekend? I don't think it's wise for us all to be staying at the house on Eyrargata, if you see what I mean. It might be confusing for him. He might think we're…'

…*A family again.* The words were left hanging, unsaid.

Ari Thór understood. Kristín was right, of course. She usually was. This time, though, he had a better solution to propose.

'I agree. But you two should stay at the house, and I'll take the hotel room.'

'No, Ari, don't be silly,' Kristín protested.

'I won't have it any other way,' Ari Thór replied warmly. 'You'll be far more comfortable at the house, and we'll find some fun things to do all together. Cook a meal, go out to dinner, whatever you like. And when you're ready for a break,

I'll take Stefnir out for a while, or I'll come over and play with him while you do your thing.'

He marked a pause.

'I might have to work a bit today. A teenage girl fell to her death from a balcony last night, and—'

'Oh, that's terrible…'

'Yes, it is. We still have a few things to clear up, but I'm hoping I'll be able to get away by the end of the day.'

Suddenly Ari Thór had a flashback to his life with Kristín and hoped he hadn't just triggered a familiar argument. He had lost count of all the times she had complained about his work and said he should put family first; he wasn't the only one who had a demanding job, was he? But to his relief, that perpetual tug-of-war now seemed to be a thing of the past. Perhaps the two of them were better off being friends, rather than a couple.

'Are you sure about the hotel?'

'A hundred percent. I can't wait to see you both,' he said, before he hung up.

Ari Thór usually preferred the Christmas holidays to the long Easter weekend, but this year, he thought, things might well be different.

6

Siglufjörður had seemed like such an inhospitable place when Ari Thór had first moved there seven years earlier, but the town had changed a lot since then. That first winter, the snowfall had been relentless and he had come close to admitting defeat, and packing up and moving back to the city. The cold and the darkness had been difficult enough to handle, but the worst thing had been the isolation. Back then, the only road into this town by the fjord that was passable in winter went through the old, narrow Strákagöng tunnel, which was often closed because of inclement weather and avalanches.

Since then, a new tunnel had opened, significantly reducing the risk of the town being cut off from the world in the dead of winter, and leading to growing numbers of visitors. Easier access had breathed new life into Siglufjörður. The old harbour was now dotted with cafés and restaurants with brightly coloured facades, and there was even a luxury waterfront hotel.

Kristín and Stefnir had arrived at the house on Eyrargata in the early afternoon. Ari Thór was thrilled to see them again, though he couldn't help but feel nostalgic. It seemed like a rare privilege to give his son a great big hug. He helped Kristín to unload their luggage, then left them to settle in while he walked over to the hotel with a duffel bag of clothes, promising to join them as soon as he'd finished work for the day.

Snowflakes were falling lightly as Ari Thór walked through the streets. There was barely a breath of wind, so the air felt cool rather than cold. The backdrop of mountains against the fjord was as stunning as always.

On the eve of a long Easter weekend that promised fairly decent weather and relatively kind temperatures – at least until the next snowstorm blew in – people from all over the country would be keen to hit the ski slopes, so it came as no surprise to Ari Thór to see so many tourists milling around the town. Traffic was heavier than usual, and parking spots would soon be a rare find. The lobby of the hotel was jammed with people waiting to check in, many of them wearing ski gear, either back early from a day on the snow, or hoping to squeeze in a few runs before nightfall.

Ari Thór joined the back of the queue behind a family of skiers with four children, and waited patiently until it was his turn to check in. There was something strange about staying in a hotel in the town where he lived, even though in many ways, he was still an outsider there. He had been readying himself to flash a sheepish smile at the fresh-faced young woman at the front desk and explain why the local police inspector was checking in to a room that had been booked by someone else, but she didn't seem to notice his uniform and only asked him for his name.

He was given a room on the first floor, at the far end of a long corridor, with a fine view of the fjord. Ari Thór knew he should get back to the station as soon as possible, but he couldn't resist the temptation to lie down for a moment. With a sigh, he stretched out on the bed and closed his eyes. The fatigue from his sleepless and eventful night was catching up with him at last.

All of a sudden, it felt like he was a world away from Siglufjörður. He wasn't used to staying in hotels. He hadn't taken a proper holiday in a long time, partly because he was wary of the expense, but also because he had no one in his life to share the experience with. Even when he and Kristín had been together, travel had been the last thing on their minds. They had both been too busy with work to go on holiday, and after Stefnir was born, even a brief getaway had been completely out of the question.

Easter weekend was shaping up to be very different from the one he had planned, so he was hoping he could carve out at least a little down time to enjoy being with his son – and Kristín. Provided that the case didn't take an unexpected turn, he could hand over the bulk of the investigation to Ögmundur, and that would take the pressure off him.

For now, the most probable explanation was that Unnur had taken her own life, in spite of her mother's insistence to the contrary. Perhaps they would never know why she had decided to jump to her death from that balcony. Unfortunate events like these often remained unexplained. Not all mysteries could be solved. Ari Thór might never have known why his own father had disappeared when Ari Thór was just a teenager if a near coincidence hadn't given him a clue.

As tragic as Unnur's death was, if the young woman had decided to commit suicide, it wasn't Ari Thór's job to find the reasons why.

Allowing his mind to wander, he decided to grant himself a few more minutes of rest. Five minutes more or less on the job would hardly change the course of the investigation, he told himself.

❅

Ari Thór woke with a start.

How long had he slept? He glanced at his phone screen:

three-quarters of an hour. It was almost a miracle that no one had called him during that time. He stood and waited for the remnants of the fog to dissipate from his mind. This short nap had given him the boost of energy he so desperately needed.

He would have to get straight back to work. Now that he was wearing the inspector's hat, he couldn't escape his responsibilities, even when he was supposed to be off duty. But with a bit of luck, he would be able to get away with a quick pit stop at the station.

❋

That morning, a team of forensic technicians had come to examine the scene, and they would soon be filing their report. Ari Thór wasn't necessarily expecting them to find anything but Unnur's prints on the balcony. But it was always best to be thorough, to make sure the slightest clue wasn't missed. He hadn't yet managed to make contact with Bjarki, the historian who lived on the first floor of the building on Aðalgata. And he still wasn't convinced that Gudjón, the artist, had told him the whole truth about his nocturnal strolls.

He hurried down the stairs and left the hotel at a brisk pace, feeling self-conscious in his uniform, as if all eyes were on him. It must be strange for all these tourists to see a police officer when all they were probably thinking about was how soon they could be on the ski slopes. One fine winter day, he would have to take little Stefnir up to the Skarðsdalur ski area and book a lesson for him with an instructor. Perhaps he could even give skiing another go himself. It felt a little embarrassing to live in a winter-sports town like Siglufjörður and not be a skier.

As Ari Thór walked the short distance to the police station, the snowflakes fell as light as feathers, melting the second they touched the ground. He would have liked to stop at the fish market on the way and pick up some dried fish to snack on, but the place was closed for renovations; the owners were expanding the store so that it could accommodate more customers. These days it seemed the town was in constant upheaval, as if the tourists and those who catered to them were taking it over one shop and restaurant at a time, like they had in the south of the country.

Fortunately, some things never changed. Ari Thór's favourite cinnamon rolls – known as *hnútar* – were still a firm fixture on the shelves of the local bakery, and were as delicious as always. He decided to stop by and pick up a whole bag for the kitchen at the station, but when he saw that people were queueing out the door he had second thoughts. *Easter tourists*, he grumbled to himself, shaking his head with a sigh. He was becoming even more resistant to change than his predecessor, Tómas.

When Ari Thór walked into the station, it was clear Ögmundur had been waiting for him.

'Where were you?' There was a hint of disdain in the rookie's voice.

Ari Thór would never have dared to take that tone with Tómas when he was the junior officer, but he decided to bite his tongue.

'I got held up. Is there any news?'

'Salvör, Unnur's mother, must have called a dozen times. She's adamant she wants to talk to you. I knew better than to give her your mobile number. I think she's just in shock and needs someone to talk to. Which is understandable.'

'I assume you tried to alleviate her concerns yourself?'

'Well, you know how it is, Ari Thór. People want to talk to a local they can trust, not a bloody outsider like me.'

Ögmundur swaggered over with a smile and gave Ari Thór a friendly punch on the shoulder. 'Charming, eh?'

Charming, indeed, Ari Thór thought. People might not think of him as an outsider at the station anymore, but that didn't necessarily mean he felt like a local. He really would have to spend some time thinking about what the hell he wanted to do with his future.

7

Just as Ari Thór was about to return Salvör's calls, the phone rang. It was the head of the forensics team.

As Ari Thór had suspected, the fingerprints collected from the balcony confirmed that the young woman had been up there, and there was no evidence to suggest anyone had accompanied her.

'If any new evidence comes to light once we've examined the samples further, I'll let you know. But it's highly unlikely,' said the man at the other end of the line.

Ari Thór immediately phoned Selma, his superior officer in Akureyri, to keep her abreast of the situation. She was only a little older than him, and had recently been promoted to superintendent.

'I gather you're dealing with a messy situation,' Selma said. 'My colleagues briefed me about it when I came in this morning. What's the latest?'

'It looks like it was suicide,' Ari Thór explained. 'By all appearances, she jumped from a balcony two floors up. The forensic evidence seems to confirm that theory, so that's what we're thinking at the moment. The victim's mother is in shock, and it's likely to cause a stir in town when the news gets out.'

Obviously, word had already started to spread, even though the story was yet to break in the media. The town seemed to have its own secret news network. Who needed technology when information could travel at lightning speed by word of mouth?

'I'm counting on you to keep a lid on things, Ari Thór,' Selma replied.

Ari Thór swore under his breath. It was his job to liaise with the local media, of course, but he really didn't want anything to get in the way of his weekend off with his son.

'If you want my opinion, this case won't go any further,' he said. 'I'm going to take a witness statement now and have a chat with the mother to see if there's any particular reason to dig deeper, but I doubt there will be.'

He was planning to delegate everything else to Ögmundur and oversee the progress of the case from a distance, so that he wouldn't have to sacrifice his weekend with Stefnir and Kristín.

'Let's tread carefully, Ari Thór,' Selma replied. 'This is a sensitive matter, so I trust you'll handle it tactfully. I don't want anything blown out of proportion. Have any journalists contacted you?'

Ari Thór cupped his hand over the phone and turned to Ögmundur. 'Have you taken any calls from the media?' he asked, keeping his voice low even though he suspected that Selma could probably hear what he was saying.

'A guy from National Radio called,' Ögmundur replied. 'I didn't tell him anything.'

Ari Thór relayed the message over the phone.

'Call him back,' Selma said. 'Tell him that a body was found overnight. It was a sudden death, but there's nothing to suggest foul play. Journalists tend to be more sensitive if they think it's suicide.'

Judging by the tone of her voice, Selma did not hold the journalist's profession in high esteem.

8

Ari Thór contacted the journalist and followed Selma's instructions about what to say. Fortunately, it seemed like the investigation wasn't making too many waves, at least for now.

After he hung up, it took him a moment to muster the courage to call Salvör, Unnur's mother. She picked up the phone on the first ring.

'Hello?'

Ari Thór could easily have walked around the corner to the woman's house to see her in person, but something made him want to keep his distance. He was reluctant to stare grief in the face – and wouldn't unless he had no choice. This was a weakness he didn't like to admit. It was something a man like Tómas would never have succumbed to.

'Hello Salvör, this is Inspector Ari Thór Arason.'

'Thank you for returning my calls.' Her voice was shaking. 'Do you … do you have any news?'

'Have you spoken to my junior officer, Ögmundur?'

'I told him I'd rather speak with you, Inspector.'

'It seems…' Ari Thór drew a sharp breath; he would have given anything to be somewhere else at that moment. 'It seems, unfortunately, that Unnur did fall to her death from the balcony. We don't know yet why that might be.'

'Surely someone was with her. There must be a witness who can tell us what happened.'

'I'm afraid that's unlikely. We were unable to find any prints other than your daughter's.' He spoke with more formality than compassion, and he felt guilty about his tone, but this call was making him feel terribly ill at ease. 'Regretfully, I don't have any more—'

'But you're not ruling it out; is that what you're saying?' Salvör interrupted. 'That there might have been someone else up there with her?'

'Yes, that does remain a possibility.'

'There's no way she could have done that. I know my daughter. Believe me, she wasn't suicidal. What about the people who live in the building? Weren't they at home? Didn't they see anything? How did she get in? It was the building on Aðalgata, where Jónína and Jóhann live, wasn't it?'

'Yes, that's right. And Bjarki, too.'

'Oh yes, old Víkingur's son. Was he not at home as well? Are you telling me no one saw anything? Or heard anything?'

While the answers to these questions would not technically reveal personal or confidential information, Ari Thór wondered how much he should reveal to the young woman's mother.

'Jónína and Jóhann were at home. I understand that they may have let her in, though we still need to confirm some of the details. And it seems that Bjarki isn't in Siglufjörður right now. I'll let you know if—'

'What? They let her into the building? Why? So they're the ones to blame, then. It's all their fault…'

'It's too soon to jump to conclusions,' Ari Thór hastily replied, silently cursing his tactless choice of words and already regretting having said too much. 'Of course, we're doing everything we can to—'

Salvör cut him off again. 'Please, you must find out what happened to my daughter. You must…'

'We will, I promise,' Ari Thór replied, though he knew it was likely that the mystery would remain forever unsolved.

'I'm trusting you, Ari Thór.' The desperation in her voice was heart-wrenching. 'I'm trusting you to do your job.'

Ari Thór took a deep breath. 'Why don't you try to get some rest, Salvör...'

'Get some rest? How the hell do you expect me to get some rest?! I'm tearing my hair out. I can't sit still for more than two minutes at a time...'

'If something comes to mind, something that might be helpful...' he ventured.

'Yes, all right,' Salvör sighed, after a brief silence. 'For pity's sake, all I want is an explanation...' she added, her voice breaking into pieces.

She hung up, leaving Ari Thór frozen in his chair.

9

Ari Thór had promised Kristín and Stefnir he would meet them at the house for a bite to eat. He was looking forward to spending some time with his three-year-old son and pretending that nothing had changed, although he knew there was no going back to the way things were. That wasn't even what he wanted, anyway. There had been plenty of good times in the years he'd spent with Kristín, but they had also gone through a lot of rough patches. That said, if she were to suggest they give it another try, he probably wouldn't turn her down, if only for Stefnir's sake.

Stepping out into the cold winter air to walk home felt like a welcome break for Ari Thór from what had been a very long day. He decided to make the most of the walk by dialling Bjarki's number again. He had been trying to reach the man to check whether he had been out of town the previous night, as Ari Thór had been led to believe. Perhaps the historian might tell him something that would cast new light on the investigation, although Ari Thór doubted he would. He was almost certain that Unnur had jumped from the balcony of her own volition. The reasons that had driven her to do so were none of his concern. But something about the conversation with Salvör earlier was nagging at him. He fully intended to keep his promise to do everything he could to find out what had happened to her daughter, so long as he didn't have to give up too much of the precious time he had to spend with his own family.

'Hello?' There was a hint of surprise in the voice of the man who answered the phone.

'Hello, is this Bjarki Víkingsson?'

'Speaking. Who is this?'

'My name is Ari Thór Arason. I'm with the Siglufjörður police.'

'The police?' Bjarki sounded puzzled. 'Has something happened? Is there a problem with my flat?'

That was interesting. The first thing the man was worried about was his home, which could suggest he had no family or friends in the area.

'No, nothing like that.'

'What's happened, then?'

'The body of a young woman ... a teenage girl, in fact, was found in the street outside your building. She fell to her death from the rooftop balcony, it seems.'

'What? Who? From the balcony? That's terrible...'

'Her name was Unnur Svavarsdóttir. Does that mean anything to you?'

'Unnur?' He fell silent for a second. 'Er, no, I don't think so. What happened?'

'I'm not in a position to share too many details, Bjarki. She fell, or perhaps she jumped. That's all I can say for now. I just wanted to let you know before you read about it in the newspaper.'

'Ah, right. Well, thank you. How tragic...'

Another moment of silence went by before he added: 'How did she get up there?'

Ari Thór hesitated. He would usually refuse to say anything, but it seemed unreasonable not to tell a resident of the building what he knew.

'Did someone else have access to your flat in your absence?'

'No, no one,' Bjarki replied. 'So, how did she get up there?'

'This isn't the kind of information we would normally share, so I would ask that you keep it to yourself…'

'Yes, of course.'

'It seems the couple who live on the ground floor buzzed the door open – without knowing who they were letting in. I don't believe they knew her personally. Unless you know more than I do about that.'

'No, I wouldn't know.'

'They've been living in the building for longer than you have, I understand.'

'Yes, a lot longer. I've only just moved in, really. My family has owned the building for years, but I've only been there a few months, on and off. I'm doing a doctorate, and writing my thesis about Icelanders who emigrated to North America, especially those who went over there from Siglufjörður. My father grew up here, you see.'

'But you don't have any family in town anymore, do you?' Ari Thór ventured.

'That's correct. How did you know?'

'I had a hunch. Tell me, Bjarki, are you in Siglufjörður at the moment?'

'No, no, I'm still in Reykjavík. I was speaking at a conference. It ended yesterday, but I've decided to treat myself to a few days off down here over Easter. Why?' he asked, deepening the tone of his voice.

After a brief hesitation, Ari Thór decided to take the plunge. 'I have to pursue every line of inquiry. After all, this did happen in your building. How should I put it? – We can't rule out the possibility that someone pushed that young woman off the balcony.'

'Pushed? I … I've…' Bjarki stammered, with none of the cool confidence of his earlier words. 'Listen, I've been in

Reykjavík for the last three days, and that's irrefutable. Just ask any of my colleagues. I was even giving a talk yesterday. I…'

'What makes you think I'm pointing the finger at you? I have no reason to doubt your word. Of course, I may ask your colleagues to corroborate your story, if necessary.'

'Very well.' Bjarki sounded relieved.

'Are you turning it into a book?' Ari Thór asked.

'A book?'

'Your thesis. It sounds like it might be an interesting topic.'

'Oh, it's fascinating. And yes, I think at least some of my research is going to be published.'

'Well, I look forward to reading it. Thank you for your time, Bjarki. I'll get in touch again if I need to.' Ari Thór ended the conversation on an assertive note. He was gaining confidence, acting more like Tómas: the man in charge, who made the decisions and carried the responsibility on his shoulders.

'Yes, of course…'

'And if anything comes to mind, Bjarki – if you happen to recall the slightest detail that might help us to understand what Unnur was doing there last night – I want you to call me right away.'

'Yes, obviously. I will.'

10

'Oh, Ari, there's no need to apologise. That sounds terrible. That girl's poor mother,' Kristín had said when he got home and told her how the day had unfolded.

Ari. He was relieved that she still felt close enough to him to drop the *Thór*, but at one time she would have said *Ari, darling.* Some days, he found himself wishing things could go back to the way they were before. He missed sipping red wine with Kristín in the evenings, talking in their kitchen about how they'd change the world, as Stefnir slept soundly upstairs.

That wish had almost come true this evening. Exhausted from the long journey, Stefnir was fast asleep in his old bed, which was now too small for him. Ari Thór had gone upstairs to check on him when he got home and had spent a long while gazing at him, thinking about all the moments in his son's life he had missed. It seemed that the distance between them was growing day by day, in spite of his son's young age and the fact he would barely remember these early years. Or perhaps that was precisely why the distance seemed so great to Ari Thór – because so many developments occur in early childhood.

Now he and Kristín were sitting at the kitchen table, just the way he had pictured in his nostalgic daydreams, only without the red wine. Other than that, it was a perfect scene, and the view from the kitchen window seemed more spectacular than ever. The mountains were bathed in a soft light, their snowy peaks sparkling in the winter sky. But Ari Thór knew things could never really be the same again. Kristín was sitting right in front of him, but this wasn't real life; it was just an illusion of it.

The conversation had felt a bit forced at the beginning, and he had apologised for having to spend so much time at work, but they soon found their groove.

'I can see you're tired, Ari,' Kristín said with a smile.

It was the same warm, gentle smile that had made him fall in love with her. Ari Thór wondered if it had melted the heart of another man since she'd been away. Had she met someone else in Sweden? He hoped not. He wanted to be the only father figure in Stefnir's life for as long as possible.

'I think you might be right,' he yawned. 'I'm sorry, I really wasn't expecting things to be so hectic while you were here.'

'Why don't you lie down next to Stefnir for a while?' Kristín suggested.

Ari Thór wanted to keep chatting with her, but the lack of sleep was catching up with him, and to be honest the idea of lying down beside his son and closing his eyes for a while was just as appealing.

'Yes, maybe I should…' he replied, the tiredness drawing out his words.

'Do you think it was suicide, Ari?' Kristín asked. 'Do you think that girl jumped?'

Ari Thór thought for a moment.

'Yes, I think that's the most likely explanation. I've seen the balcony; any suggestion it was an accident would be a bit far-fetched, if you ask me. I can't see how anyone could fall from there unintentionally.'

'Unless someone…' Kristín left her thought hanging.

Ari Thór looked up at her. 'I really hope that's not what happened,' he replied.

'But knowing you, you've given the possibility some thought, haven't you?' She smiled again.

Kristín was right, of course: he was considering all the

people he had encountered so far in connection with Unnur's death as potential suspects, just in case. First there was Gudjón, the artist who had discovered the body; then there were Jóhann and Jónína, the couple who lived on the ground floor of the building. He couldn't rule out Salvör, Unnur's mother ... or Bjarki, the historian who lived upstairs and had said he was away when it happened.

Obviously, the list of potential suspects might be longer. Who did Unnur see on a day-to-day basis? Who knew her well? Friends, classmates, perhaps. Or her father. Ari Thór's thoughts began to wander.

'Well, we can't rule anything out, you know,' he said, stifling a yawn.

'Oh, Ari, I think it's time for you to close your eyes for a while. I'm going to let Stefnir nap for another half an hour, so why don't you make the most of it and curl up beside him?'

Ari Thór stood up.

'Good idea. I'll see you in a bit.'

He climbed the stairs and tiptoed into the master bedroom as quietly as he could. Easing his head down gently on the pillow, Ari Thór stretched out on top of the covers and turned onto his side to gaze at his son sleeping soundly in the little bed beside his. He was so handsome. And he had grown so much. It had been a few months since their last visit. It was one thing for them to talk on the phone sometimes and enjoy the occasional video chat, when Stefnir was in a good mood, but it was always a treat to see his son in person and hold him in his arms.

Ari Thór reached out and placed his hand gently over his son's. Then he closed his eyes and let himself drift into dreamland, where everything was always perfect, just the way it was meant to be.

GOOD FRIDAY

11

'Hello … Ari Thór…?'

They hadn't spoken in ages, but he recognised her voice immediately.

He and Ugla had met during his first winter in Siglufjörður. There had been some chemistry between them, and it might have developed into a serious relationship if Ari Thór hadn't neglected to tell her he still had a girlfriend back in Reykjavík. Since then, on the rare occasions they had run into each other, Ugla had barely given him the time of day.

His brief encounter with Ugla had spelled the beginning of the end for Ari Thór and Kristín, who eventually separated, although they did stay together for a number of years and had a child together – little Stefnir.

Ugla was calling him on his mobile. She must have held on to his number all this time, because he liked as few people as possible to know it.

Ari Thór hesitated for a second, not because he didn't want to speak to her, but because hearing her voice was like travelling back in time, to the moment when they had first met seven years ago, not long after he had arrived in Siglufjörður. Something between him and Ugla had clicked straight away. They had really connected, to the point where Ari Thór had allowed himself to forget all about Kristín for a time. Hearing her voice now filled him with a curious sense of excitement all over again.

'Ugla,' he said warmly. 'Hi. It's nice to hear your voice.'

'Thanks. Same here,' she replied, after an uncomfortably long pause that made her words sound less than convincing.

'How are you?' Ari Thór asked. 'To what do I owe the pleasure?'

He knew that she had recently left her job in the fishing industry and was working somewhere else. A doctor had bought the old Siglufjörður schoolhouse, which had been derelict for years, and turned it into a private nursing home; Ugla had found a job there as a carer. Ari Thór had heard the news by word of mouth and didn't know much about the place, other than the fact that it promised to be a lucrative business. Apparently the doctor had bought the building for a song, and if it attracted enough residents, the establishment would receive significant government funding.

'I'm fine,' Ugla replied. 'Is this a bad time for me to call?'

'No, not at all.'

'It's just that … I wanted to talk to you about the girl who died yesterday. I heard about it on the news, and…'

'Did you know her?' Ari Thór asked.

'No. Well, I don't think so. I'd never heard her name before. She was nineteen, wasn't she? I don't really hang around with people her age.'

'I understand,' Ari Thór replied, leaving her to get to the point in her own time.

'Anyway, I don't know if what I'm going to say is connected at all, but you never know. I wanted to talk to you before I told anyone else, Ari Thór. I know we haven't been in touch much since…'

Much. Ari Thór couldn't help but smile to himself. *Not at all* would have been closer to the truth. She had flown into a fury when he had told her that he had a girlfriend. And he could hardly blame her. She had then closed herself off completely and had barely said another word to him. But now, the warmth in her voice suggested that her anger had softened.

'Yes, I know,' Ari Thór replied simply.

'Maybe we can talk about that later,' Ugla said softly.

The sound of her voice set butterflies fluttering in his stomach, just like Kristín's had earlier. For goodness' sake, he was a grown man – why was he reacting like a lovestruck teenager? Besides, now really wasn't the time to flirt with fantasies of Ugla. Not in the middle of an investigation, and especially not while Kristín was in town.

'I wondered when you might be able to come and see me. I'd rather explain this in person than over the phone.' She fell silent for a moment before adding: 'It's probably nothing, and it might not have anything to do with that girl, but ... I think it's best you know about it, all the same.'

'Of course. I've got some time right now, if you're available.'

Ugla hesitated for a second. 'Er, yes, OK. I'm at work. Can you meet me here?'

'I'll be there soon. It's only a short walk.'

'Oh, I forgot to tell you: I've changed jobs. I'm working at the new nursing home now, the one in the old schoolhouse.'

'I know,' Ari Thór replied reflexively. Perhaps it was a subconscious way of letting her know he hadn't forgotten about her.

'Ah, OK. Well now's a good time, actually. I'll be on my own here for at least another hour. The doctor's gone out, and I'd rather he didn't know I was talking to the police about one of the residents. Especially as this might just turn out to be a silly suspicion of mine...'

'All right. I'm on my way now.' Ari Thór ended the call.

I'd rather he didn't know I was talking to the police about one of the residents, she had said. That was certainly enough to pique Ari Thór's curiosity. But most of all, he was looking forward to seeing Ugla again.

12

Tómas used to speak fondly of his school days, Ari Thór recalled. 'It's a real shame they had to close the old schoolhouse,' his former boss would often say, when they passed the building. Ari Thór smiled, remembering how much he had enjoyed working with Tómas. They had made a good team, and Tómas had been the trustworthy authority figure Ari Thór could turn to. Ari Thór had been in the inspector's position for a while now, and although he appreciated the bigger salary and the greater respect his new title commanded, he found the work itself far more solitary than he'd expected.

When Ugla called, Ari Thór was still in his room at the hotel, after enjoying a good night's sleep. In spite of being so busy, he had managed to spend a good stretch of time with Kristín and Stefnir the previous evening, after he had woken from a much-needed nap beside his son. He had taken some calls from the media, and the young woman's death had been reported on the TV news that evening, although no details had been mentioned. But news travelled fast in a small town, and soon everyone would be talking about what had happened. It wouldn't be long before rumours started to fly.

Ari Thór pulled on his parka and strode purposefully out of the hotel. He walked through the park in front of the town hall, up the hill beside the church and past the primary school where Stefnir would have been going, if things had worked out differently between his parents. Then he turned on to Hlídarvegur, the street on which the old schoolhouse stood.

It was a bitterly cold morning, and the first snowflakes of

the day were already starting to fall. The wind was light – an early sign of the coming storm. A good dump of snow was expected over Easter, much to the delight of the skiers who had descended on Siglufjörður. However, a major blizzard was forecast to blow in towards the end of the long weekend, bringing with it treacherous whiteout conditions.

Ari Thór had taken to the slopes a few times, but he was still very much a beginner. He knew that people would never really think of him as a local if he didn't at least pretend to like skiing, so he was persevering, and every time he went, he felt like he was making a little progress.

The old schoolhouse was an imposing building. Painted red all over, it had clearly been spruced up since the change of ownership. However, there was nothing on the outside of the building to suggest it now housed a private care home. If it weren't for the air of quiet and calm, it could still have been a school.

Ugla was waiting for Ari Thór at the door when he arrived. He was about to shake her hand when she pulled him into a hug.

'It's good to see you, Ari Thór,' she said.

'Nice to see you too,' he replied. 'It's been a while.'

'Far too long,' she smiled. 'Follow me. He's upstairs.'

The interior of the building was bright, airy and spotlessly clean. As the sound of a distant radio floated towards his ears, it struck Ari Thór how different this private nursing home was from publicly run facilities. It wasn't just the decor. There was a sense of spaciousness to the place.

'So you're holding the fort, then?' he asked.

'Yes,' Ugla replied. 'I'm on my own at the moment. It's usually pretty quiet around here in the daytime, so most of the time, there are only two of us. Dóra and me. We take turns doing the night shift with Hersir, and a volunteer from town lends us a hand. Hersir is the doctor who runs the place,' she added, as Ari Thór nodded.

'At the moment we have four rooms and each of those can accommodate two residents. There are four more rooms upstairs, but those aren't ready yet. The budget's been a bit tight, you see, but work on those has just started again. If there aren't enough residents in the home, Hersir can't afford the renovation work, you see. We were full to capacity, but we have some spaces at the moment. I think Hersir's been negotiating with some of the other local authorities, seeing if they'll channel more residents our way.'

'Are you happy here?' Ari Thór asked.

Ugla looked at him. She seemed surprised by the question. 'Very. I just hope Hersir manages to make a go of this place. I'm thinking of going back to college to study nursing, you know.'

'Really?' Ari Thór asked. 'When?'

'Maybe in the autumn. I've gained some good experience working here.'

For some mysterious reason, Ari Thór didn't like the idea that Ugla might be leaving Siglufjörður. Admittedly, they hadn't properly spoken to each other in years, but there was still some sort of invisible thread connecting them, he felt. A fraying thread that he had neglected to mend. Ari Thór tried to shake these idle thoughts from his mind. Nothing was going to happen between him and Ugla. Nor between him and Kristín, for that matter.

'Is this Hersir the only doctor here?' Ari Thór asked. 'I don't suppose he's looking for someone to share the load with?'

In spite of everything that had happened, he couldn't resist the temptation to discreetly enquire about a potential job opportunity for Kristín. If she were to find work here, they could at least live in the same town, even if their relationship was beyond repair. And Ari Thór would get to see his son every day.

'To be honest, I think it's still too complicated for Hersir to think about hiring someone else. He and his wife have put their life savings into this venture. It's cost a fortune, because the whole building needed renovating. But they've done a good job. It's such a nice place to work. Although, if property prices were a bit higher, I'd wonder whether it wouldn't be more worth their while to turn the place into flats and put them up for sale. That said, Hersir seems to be set on making the nursing home profitable. Oh, I forgot to ask: do you know him?'

They were chatting in the middle of the upstairs corridor now, and Ari Thór could see that several of the doors leading off it were open. The volume of the radio he had heard earlier had grown louder. It must be coming from one of the residents' rooms, he thought. For Ari Thór, the sound of Rás 1 drifting over the airwaves brought back memories of being at his grandmother's house as a boy. He had gone to live with her after his mother died and his father disappeared. Back then, the old 'steam machine', as they used to call the Icelandic public radio station, would be on all day in the background, and Ari Thór had grown quite fond of the formal yet reassuring drone of the hosts' voices.

'I've heard his name,' he replied. In small towns as remote as this, everyone knew who the doctors, police officers and pastors were. They were the last bastions of a society that used to revolve around these institutions.

'He's the kind of man you can count on in times of need. A good man, with a nice bedside manner.' Ugla smiled.

She obviously liked her boss and thought he was good with the residents, Ari Thór thought. Then it dawned on him that there might be something more to her relationship with Hersir. The thought gave him a sinking feeling in his stomach. But it was unlikely to be the case, he reasoned. Hersir was a married man – and much older than Ugla, for that matter.

'Hávardur's in this room here,' Ugla said, pointing to a closed door. 'I think he's sleeping at the moment. He's well over eighty. He might be losing his marbles, but a lot of the time he's surprisingly clear-headed, which is why I was so worried, you know...'

'What were you worried about, exactly?'

'What he wrote.'

Ari Thór still didn't know what Ugla was talking about.

'Dóra and I were talking about the teenage girl who died,' Ugla continued. 'We were in Hávardur's room. He likes to have company, you see, even when he's sleeping. We were just gossiping, really, saying things like "oh, the poor girl, what a terrible thing to happen..."'

Ugla was scattering her words about now; something seemed to be weighing on her.

'Dóra, my colleague ... she knew the girl's mother a bit. Anyway, Hávardur came to and asked us what we were talking about. Turns out he's lived here his whole life and he knew the girl's grandfather – everyone knows everyone here in Siglufjörður, not that I need to tell you that. So we told him what had happened. We didn't think there was any harm in it. We didn't mean to cause him any grief, you know?'

Ari Thór nodded, keen to hear what she was going to say.

'But neither of us was expecting him to react the way he did. He got really agitated and asked if she was really dead.

And then it was like he was trying to tell us something. It was really disturbing, Ari Thór. Part of me thought he must just be confused. Sometimes, he's perfectly lucid, but other times it's like he's locked inside his own mind. Hersir is a specialist in geriatric medicine, so naturally—'

'Would it help if I talked to him?' Ari Thór cut in. 'Hávardur, I mean.'

Ugla paused, unsure what to answer. 'Well, I'm not sure that would be wise. It's hard to know if you're going to catch him at a good time and actually get through to him. But I did want to show you something...'

She took a step towards the door, then stopped, hesitant to go any further.

'He likes to sketch, you see,' Ugla said, almost as if she was drawing out the suspense. 'And he used to paint a lot when he was younger. He was quite famous, actually. You've probably seen some of his art without realising it. He's very talented. There's always a sketch pad and some coloured pencils and markers, that sort of thing, beside his bed. Just in case he wakes up and feels the urge, he says. And this morning, when I came in to check on him, this is what I saw...'

She opened the door.

13

There were two beds in the room, but only the one closest to the window was occupied. Hávardur was asleep. Or at least, he wasn't moving. And on the wall behind him, he had scrawled three words with a blood-red marker:

She was murdered.

Over and over again.

A shiver ran down Ari Thór's spine. He ventured forward for a closer look at the writing on the wall. The words were scribbled, and some were almost illegible, but the message was clear. The wall was a picture of the chaos inside the mind of a troubled man. It was almost completely covered in those same three words: *She was murdered.*

Did Hávardur know something? Had he known Unnur as well as her grandparents? Had the elderly man received any visitors since the body was discovered?

'It's … very curious,' was all Ari Thór said.

'See why I thought it was unsettling?' Ugla replied. 'I was going to try and clean the wall, but I wanted you to have a look at it first. Obviously, what you see could simply be the ravings of a deranged mind. But he wrote those words in the night, after our conversation about the girl who died. It's creepy. It's as if he knew something, somehow…'

'Based on what you know about his mental health, should we be taking this seriously?' Ari Thór asked.

'That's a question for Hersir to answer. I'm no specialist, but like I said, he always seems to be drifting in and out of his own little world. Sometimes he just talks gibberish. But often, what he says makes perfect sense.'

Ari Thór wished he could brush this off as nonsense and tell Ugla to scrub the wall clean if she wanted to. He wished he could reassure her – and himself – that what they saw were the deluded scribbles of a loopy old man. That would make things so much easier.

It was Easter weekend, and Kristín and little Stefnir were waiting for him at home. The last thing Ari Thór wanted to do was pursue a new angle in an investigation he'd rather not be leading in the first place.

Realistically, he couldn't consider this a clue, let alone a lead. Hávardur was senile. And if there was any connection between these words on the wall and the teenage girl who had died, it was loose at best. The simplest thing would be to pretend that Ugla hadn't even called him.

But he knew in his gut that something wasn't right here. He took a few photos of the wall with his phone, then turned to Ugla.

'Could I ask you to wait until I've spoken with Hersir before you clean the wall?' he asked.

'Of course. No problem at all. He's supposed to be back soon. I doubt he's thrilled to be holed up here this weekend though. Everyone wants to be out on the ski slopes. You could always go knock on his door if you like. He and his wife live near here.'

'I'm not sure that will be necessary, but perhaps you should give me the address anyway,' Ari Thór mumbled, more to himself than to Ugla.

Ugla hazarded a glance at the elderly man and seemed relieved to see that he was still fast asleep. Then she placed a cautious hand on Ari Thór's shoulder. It was time for them to step outside the room.

'Let's talk more somewhere else,' she said. 'I'd rather we didn't wake him up.'

They went down to the staff kitchen and sat at an old wooden table. Ugla put the kettle on.

'If my memory serves me well, you're a tea drinker, aren't you?'

Ari Thór smiled. 'Black tea would be lovely, thanks.'

Truth be told, he had acquired a taste for coffee, but he chose to keep that to himself.

'Did you ever get into skiing in the end?' Ugla asked, while she waited for the kettle to boil.

'Not really,' he replied. 'To be honest, the idea of it still freaks me out a bit. I'd rather not break a leg if I can help it.'

'Oh, it's so much fun, Ari Thór. Skiing's one of the reasons I've stayed in this town for so long.'

One of the reasons.

'Weren't you saying you wanted to go back to university, though? That would mean moving somewhere else, wouldn't it?'

It was a pleasure to be with Ugla, Ari Thór realised. The conversation flowed so naturally, as if they had seen each other just yesterday. Maybe she had forgiven him, he thought. Maybe, just maybe, they might pick up where they left off. It was a tiny glimmer of hope and he had to admit that the thought hadn't even really crossed his mind before now.

'To study nursing, yes,' she replied. 'It's a field that really interests me, and I think I'd make a good nurse.'

'I don't doubt that for a second. Are you still living in the same flat – that lovely place on Nordurgata?' Ari Thór asked, even though he already knew the answer.

'Yes. I was renting it at first, but I own it now. You remember the old house I inherited a few years ago when you and I … before we fell out of touch? I ended up selling that to a lawyer from Reykjavík, and I used the proceeds to pay off the mortgage on the flat. That house was far too big for me to live in on my own, anyway.'

Surely it was no accident that she had mentioned that. *She still lived alone.* Ari Thór knew that at one point she had been seeing a man at the company where she had worked, but the relationship hadn't lasted long.

'How are the piano lessons going?' Ugla asked, with a hint of mischief in her voice.

She had taught him for a while, but the lessons had ended as abruptly as their brief flirtation with a relationship.

'I have to admit I've neglected my piano-playing a bit,' Ari Thór replied. 'I still have a decent grasp of the basics, though. Sometimes I'll sit down at the piano at home and try to play something, but … I think I'd like to start making more of an effort.'

'I've stopped teaching actually. I don't think it was good for me,' Ugla said, pouring water over a tea bag and handing the mug to Ari Thór.

'I still have my piano, though,' she continued. 'I suppose I could make an exception and give you a few more lessons to get you back on track. But I should warn you: my hourly rate is higher than it used to be,' she said with a coy smile.

14

As Ari Thór walked away from the nursing home, he noticed the streets in town were quite a bit busier than usual.

The snow was falling thick and fast now. At this rate, the whole town would be blanketed in white by nightfall. The winter storms didn't bother Ari Thór as much as they used to. Now that the new tunnel was open, Siglufjörður didn't feel as remote as it once did. With two roads connecting the town to the rest of the country now, the chances of being cut off from the world were far slimmer than before. Ari Thór shuddered to think that for many years the notoriously narrow Strákagöng tunnel, often blocked by avalanches in the thick of winter, had been the only way in – or out.

Ari Thór decided to give Kristín a call while he was walking. 'Hi there,' he said. 'Do you want to meet up at lunchtime?'

'Yes. Or earlier, if you can,' Kristín replied. 'Stefnir's keen to see you. We could take him tobogganing. It would be nice to make the most of this snow before the wind starts to blow it all around.'

'I should be able to get away soon,' Ari Thór said.

He was hesitant to tell her that the investigation was going to be taking up more of his time than he had thought this weekend. Especially as he still wasn't sure there was anything suspicious about the young woman's death.

In the past, calls like this would have triggered an argument. Back then, he had often been too busy with work to spend time with her, but so had she. But given how little time they had together this weekend to spend with their son, Ari Thór was anxious to avoid conflict.

'Why don't I meet you at home as soon as I'm free?' he suggested.

'No, come and find us at the bakery instead. We're just heading out for some fresh air.'

Ari Thór agreed and hung up, and heading back towards the town centre, he decided to pay Hersir a visit after all.

It didn't take him long to get to the doctor's house. Painted ox-blood red, the old wooden building sat in what in the summertime would be a pretty garden. There was a narrow path leading from the pavement to the front door. Ari Thór remembered that this house had been in a state of ruin when he first moved to the town. Now it stood tall and proud as it carried its old-fashioned charm into the future. This was no small house, and the architecture was striking. It was impressive without being intimidating.

The doctor's house was a sign of the times. More and more properties around town were being brought back to life – renovated from top to bottom, as Siglufjörður embraced a new era. Now the ski slopes above the town were well and truly back in vogue, and restaurants and hotels were popping up all over the place to cater to the influx of people from down south who had realised the benefits of owning a cabin in the far north for their summer holidays. When Ari Thór had first arrived here, houses were changing hands for next to nothing. Since then, property prices had been steadily increasing, although they were still a far cry from the cost of places in the nation's capital.

A few years ago, people had told Ari Thór that the economic growth the banking industry had brought to the country had never reached Siglufjörður. But now tourism was making its mark here, though there was still room for progress. And the locals seemed happy. There was an air of spring about the place this weekend – at least in the streets and the businesses around town – but one breath of the air outside was enough to remind Ari Thór that winter was not yet ready to release its icy grip.

Ari Thór hadn't called ahead to announce his visit. He knocked at the door, and Hersir opened the door almost immediately.

'Well, if it isn't the inspector himself!' he exclaimed, with a smile that soon faded into a graver expression. 'Is everything all right? Has something happened?'

'Nothing that concerns you directly, Hersir. There's no need to worry. Do you mind if I come in? I'd like to ask you a few questions about one of your residents, if that's all right.'

'Of course.' The doctor stepped aside and closed the door behind Ari Thór.

The house was warm and inviting, like a holiday cabin, with an open plan that blended the kitchen, dining area and living room into one airy space.

Ari Thór accepted the invitation to sit at the kitchen table and didn't waste any time on pleasantries. 'This is about Hávardur.'

Sitting across from him, Hersir tilted his head slightly. 'Oh, really?' He seemed genuinely surprised.

'How should I put this … Last night, it appears that he scrawled some troubling words on the wall of his room after … a conversation with your employees about the teenage girl who died early yesterday morning. I understand that he knew her family.'

'What do you mean, scrawled on the wall?' Hersir retorted.

'And how would you know that, anyway? I'm not sure where you're going with this.'

Ari Thór realised that what he was about to say might get Ugla into trouble, but the damage was already done.

'Ugla phoned me this morning,' he explained. 'She thought the writing might have something to do with the teenager's death.'

'The teenager's death? But how could Hávardur…' Hersir caught himself before he said any more. 'What did he write, exactly? Ugla should have called me to tell me about this…' He shook his head.

'She was murdered,' Ari Thór replied.

'What?' the doctor gasped.

'That's what Hávardur wrote on the wall. "She was murdered". Over and over again.'

Hersir was lost for words.

'I'm not saying these two things are necessarily connected, but you have to admit it seems strange,' Ari Thór continued.

'Very strange,' said Hersir. 'The poor man is very ill. He has serious dementia.'

The doctor was clearly irked to have found out what had happened at the home from the police, rather than his own staff.

'Try to put yourself in Ugla's shoes,' Ari Thór said, as if he had read the man's mind. 'She was shocked by what she had seen, and her instinct was to call me. We know each other quite well, and news about a young woman's death travels quickly. It's early days, but so far all the evidence seems to suggest it was suicide. Still, I have to follow up every lead to see if there's the slightest possibility of a crime having been committed.'

'Of course. The poor girl. Such a terrible way to go…' Hersir sighed.

'Can you tell me a bit more about Hávardur?' Ari Thór pressed. 'Could he have written those words consciously?'

The doctor leaned back in his chair and rubbed his temples in thought. 'I don't know what to tell you, Ari Thór. He's a senile old man. Sometimes what he says makes sense, and other times it's like he's talking to himself. If you ask me, in all likelihood...'

Hersir hesitated.

'In all likelihood, this means nothing at all. But surely you don't think somebody killed her, do you?'

'No, I don't think so,' Ari Thór replied. 'I can't imagine why anyone would want to hurt her. She was only nineteen years old...'

Suddenly, a shrill female voice rang out from above them. 'Hersir!'

A woman who looked to be around forty appeared at the top of the stairs. 'Oh, I'm sorry, I didn't know we had company,' she said with a smile as she came downstairs and extended a hand for Ari Thór to shake. 'I don't believe we've met. My name's Rósa. I'm Hersir's wife.'

Ari Thór stood up and shook her hand. 'Inspector Ari Thór Arason. I'm with the Siglufjörður police.'

'Of course, I know who you are,' Rósa replied, before turning to her husband. 'Is everything all right, darling?'

'Yes, it's just one of the residents. Hávardur ... you know who I'm talking about?'

'Is he dead? Oh, the poor man. And with him gone there'll be no one left in that room...'

'No, no, he's just had a little episode. Apparently he's scribbled something all over the walls. I'll have to go over there and have a look,' Hersir replied.

'Would you mind if I had a word with him?' Ari Thór asked.

'Well, I'll have to get the family's permission, of course. His son lives in town. I'll give him a call first, if that's all right with you.'

Ari Thór nodded.

'But I doubt Hávardur will have anything useful to tell you,' Hersir added. 'Lately it's been very hard to make any sense of what he says.'

Ari Thór was ready to take his leave. He had remained standing after getting up to shake Rósa's hand. There was no reason to prolong this visit any further.

'Please let me know when I can come and see Hávardur,' he said. 'There's no harm in speaking to him, even if what he says amounts to nothing much.'

Now Hersir stood as well. 'Of course, we'll find a time over the weekend. I imagine you're going to be around over Easter?'

Ari Thór smiled. 'Of course. Like everyone else, it seems.'

'Perhaps we'll see you on the ski slopes, in that case. Rósa and I intend to get up there and enjoy the snow as much as we can.'

15

The bakery wasn't what it used to be. When Ari Thór had first arrived in Siglufjörður, it was just a tiny, old-fashioned hole in the wall. But with increasing numbers of tourists descending on the town almost all year round, the owners had done a lot of work to expand the space and turn their modest business into a thriving café. The times were changing, and while Ari Thór occasionally felt nostalgic for the cosy old bakery, he still enjoyed stepping into this bustling new place. He was glad the owners hadn't stopped filling the display cases with their good old cinnamon rolls, although it was becoming a challenge to get his hands on the sweet treats, as they tended to sell out more quickly. If he was out of luck, he would usually fall back on one of the delicious *sírópskökur* – one of the delicious syrup cakes with pink frosting and a hint of liquorice the locals said were a Siglufjörður delicacy.

As a young boy, Ari Thór had always thought Good Friday was the most sacred day of the entire year. Everything was closed, and his parents even forbade him from playing cards. The only thing he had been allowed to do to pass the time was read, until the family sat down in the evening to watch the special Easter TV programmes aired by the Icelandic National Broadcasting Service. Nowadays, Good Friday seemed to be much like any other day. The bakery was open, and all the tables were packed with customers wearing ski gear. Outside, the snowflakes were still gently falling. As soon as Ari Thór stepped inside and the smell of baking and freshly ground coffee filled his nostrils, it felt like he was wrapped up in a warm, cosy blanket.

Kristín was sitting at a table in the corner, buttering a slice of bread and chatting to Stefnir. She looked up and smiled, and the little boy craned his neck to see, without getting out of his seat. There had been a time when Stefnir might have jumped up and flung himself into his father's arms, but he had grown more distant since Kristín had taken him to live in Sweden with her. Even though things between him and Kristín were amicable, Ari Thór found that Stefnir had grown shy and less talkative around his father. He didn't know how to go about changing that, short of moving to Sweden himself so that he could be more present in his son's life.

This was just a temporary situation, he kept telling himself; Kristín had promised to return to Iceland once she had completed her master's. But that was little consolation for Ari Thór, because it was a long course and he knew how important the first few years of a child's life were, not to mention how quickly they went by. Perhaps he should have insisted on Stefnir staying longer with him this time. He had no desire to create conflict with Kristín, though, nor to uproot his son from his life with his mother. Ari Thór was confident they would end up finding the right balance.

In any case, he wasn't about to spoil the weekend by thinking about that. They were here together right now, and that was all that mattered.

'Hi.' Ari Thór hugged them both in turn.

Kristín was nursing a cup of coffee and Stefnir was sipping orange juice through a straw between mouthfuls of doughnut.

'I'll go and order something,' Ari Thór said, checking they didn't want anything else before joining the queue at the counter.

His phone rang while he was waiting.

'Hi, it's Ugla.'

'Oh, hi,' he replied, looking over his shoulder to make sure Kristín was out of earshot. He didn't want to explain himself to her. Not that he should have to.

'Hersir just called. He's on his way over to the care home. He asked me to clean the wall. Is that all right with you?'

'Yes, of course.'

She let a brief moment of silence pass between them before she asked: 'I wondered if you might like to come over to my place for a coffee. I'm around all weekend.'

Ari Thór's heart fluttered. But he didn't want to have to say anything to Kristín about Ugla; nor did he want to risk messing things up with Ugla, just as they were starting to get to know each other again, by mentioning Kristín to her.

'I'd love to,' he replied. 'Er, I'll call you if I get a moment to myself. I'm up to my eyes in work, but you never know.'

He ended the call and when he got to the front of the queue, ordered his usual steaming-hot tea. There were no cinnamon rolls left. The customer before him had just bought the last one.

16

'Tell me about Unnur.'

Ari Thór was sitting with Salvör, the dead girl's mother, in her living room. All the lights were off. The only source of brightness came from the window.

Kristín had taken Stefnir to the playground, so Ari Thór had decided to stop in at the police station. There had been multiple messages from Salvör waiting for him. He had already been planning to pay her a visit, if only to quiet the doubt that Ugla had instilled in his mind. Granted, Hersir had warned him not to take too seriously the words the elderly man had scrawled on the wall of his room, but the message was so disturbing – and potentially relevant to an active case – that Ari Thór had no choice but to investigate further.

'Thank you for coming to see me,' Salvör said, even though she'd said it already. Her eyes were bloodshot, and her features were drawn and haggard. 'The Reverend Eggert has been a godsend, keeping me company. I've no one else to turn to, with no family in the area. My sister lives overseas. She's trying to get some time off work to fly home and see me.'

'What about Unnur's father?' Ari Thór asked.

'He lives in America. He caught a flight back to Reykjavík last night, so he should be here soon. We're divorced.'

The situation felt all too familiar to Ari Thór: mother and child in one country, and father in another. For a split second, he was tempted to ask Salvör about Unnur's relationship with her father. That would give him a window into how things might evolve for him and Stefnir. He thought better of it. 'I'll need his details, so I can ask him some questions when he arrives,' was all he said.

'Of course,' Salvör nodded.

'But I'd like you to tell me a bit about your daughter,' Ari Thór insisted. 'If that's not too difficult for you.'

Salvör took a deep breath, as if trying to gather her strength. Then she wiped a tear from her cheek and lifted her gaze to meet his. 'Oh, Unnur, she's … she was so kind, and thoughtful. She was never any trouble at all, and I never had to worry about her. She worked hard at school. She was often top of her class.'

'I presume she went to the high school in Ólafsfjördur, then?' School in Iceland was compulsory until the age of sixteen, when students completed lower secondary school. Those wanting to pursue higher education first had to study for a further three or four years.

'Yes. We had talked about sending her to Reykjavík for her upper secondary education, but in the end she decided to stay here, close to home. I don't think she was ready to spread her wings and be more independent than she already was. We were still very, very close, mind you. We've always got on well. She seemed to like staying at home, and I certainly enjoyed having her around. I work at the fish company. Director of finance. It's a good job, and the salary is more than generous, so we lead … we led quite a comfortable life here. Siglufjörður is a lovely place to live if you like feeling close to nature. There's nothing quite like the sense of calm around here, down by the fjord. When this is what you're used to, the idea of living in a city like Reykjavík is hard to fathom.'

She fell silent and closed her eyes, but it was too late to stop the tears from coursing down her cheeks.

'Did you grow up here?' Ari Thór asked. 'The two of you, I mean.'

'Yes. I grew up in this very house, actually. My parents lived here as long as they were together. Sadly, they passed away some years ago – they had me quite late in life. Anyway, Svavar and I – that's my ex-husband – we lived here together for a long time after that. He came up to Siglufjörður for work. He was a ship's captain. Then ... well, he ended up falling for another woman, in Reykjavík. She emigrated to America, and he followed her.'

Ari Thór detected a certain bitterness in her voice. It was obvious that she harboured some unresolved anger towards her ex-husband, even though, by all appearances, she seemed to be able to talk about her marriage and divorce quite comfortably. But the time had come to bring up a more delicate matter.

'Did Unnur have ... someone in her life?' he asked.

Salvör was quick to react. 'Do you mean a boyfriend? No. She had plenty of other things to do with her time. Plus, she would have told me if she was seeing anyone. She wasn't in a hurry to do those kinds of things. She had her life ahead of her,' Salvör stammered, as her eyes welled up again with tears. 'She had her sights set on going to university. She was focusing on her studies. Unnur was such a beautiful girl, she could have had anyone she wanted. But she just wasn't interested in boys. As far as she was concerned, all that could wait. She was very conscientious about doing well at school. That was always what mattered the most to her.'

Salvör paused, then added with a whisper: 'She was so intelligent ... There was no one smarter than her...'

'What can you tell me about her friends?' Ari Thór asked.

'She didn't have many,' Salvör replied. 'To my knowledge,

she only really had one close friend: Sara. Unnur didn't go out much. That wasn't her thing. Like I said, she was the quiet, studious type. She always preferred to stay at home with me.'

'Was she an only child?'

'Yes and no. She was my only child, but she had half-siblings thanks to her father. They live with him in the States.'

'Is she in touch with them?'

'No, not really. Boston is a world away from here...'

'Tell me, Salvör, did she drink at all?'

'She was no saint, if that's what you're asking. Yes, of course she'd tasted alcohol and seemed to like it, but she enjoyed it responsibly. Just the odd glass every now and then. She wasn't dependent or anything. I don't drink much at home, and there's no history of alcoholism in the family. Not on my side, and not on Svavar's either.'

'I imagine she wasn't into taking drugs? I'm sorry, but I have to ask,' Ari Thór explained.

'Of course she wasn't.'

'Because even in our quiet little town, there's a bit of dealing that goes on, just like everywhere else, and I know some teenagers have been tempted to experiment. Are you absolutely sure she hadn't somehow fallen in with the wrong crowd?'

'Absolutely,' Salvör replied, without a second's hesitation. 'Listen, Ari Thór, I know people must be thinking my daughter got herself into some sort of trouble and decided to take her own life; it would be easy to jump to that conclusion. But there's no way I can ever believe that,' she added, choking back a tear.

Ari Thór decided not to mention Hávardur. For now, it was best to wait. He had no proof that what the elderly man had scrawled on the wall was actually connected to Unnur's death. That didn't mean it wasn't suspicious, though. And there was something about this conversation that seemed off as well. If her mother was to be believed, Unnur Svavarsdóttir was a model student and a conscientious daughter. An exemplary teenager with no problems whatsoever.

But Ari Thór knew from experience that appearances could be deceptive. Nothing was ever completely black or white. Unnur must have had some secrets. Everyone had a darker side they'd rather keep to themselves. The question was whether those secrets could have driven her to suicide – or driven someone else to murder.

'Do you have any idea what might have happened, Salvör?' Ari Thór asked, hesitantly.

She let a moment pass in silence, then opened her mouth to reply between sobs, 'I don't have a clue. I just can't comprehend this at all. It's all I can think about. I haven't slept a wink in twenty-four hours. The only thing I can bring myself to imagine is that someone pushed her, that someone killed my poor little girl. And I don't understand why anyone would ever want to do that. The not knowing is killing me.'

Ari Thór didn't know what to say, so allowed a silence to sit between them.

The table in front of Ari Thór was covered with old photo albums, some of which were open to snapshots of Unnur. The room was so dark and gloomy, he had to strain his eyes to make out her features. He didn't recall having seen her on any of the rare occasions he had been called to deal with teenagers causing trouble in town. It was always the same few bad apples, and Unnur didn't seem to be part of that crowd.

'Did she keep a diary?' he asked, breaking the silence.

Salvör gave a start, as if she was lost in her thoughts and

had forgotten he was still there. 'What? Sorry, I was miles away. What were you saying?'

'I asked you if Unnur had a journal that she wrote in.'

'No, I don't think so,' Salvör replied. 'Actually, I'm quite sure she didn't. If she did, she would have told me. She did have one of those day planners, though. But I think she only used that for school. You know, keeping track of her homework, that sort of thing. I'd be happy to show you that, if you want to see it.'

'Yes, I do, thank you,' Ari Thór replied.

Salvör stood up. 'It's in her room. Follow me.'

Unnur's bedroom was a good size. Other than the unmade bed, it looked quite tidy. The shelves on the wall were filled with novels and children's books. There was a pile of school textbooks beside a laptop on her desk. And what looked like a school backpack was sitting on the chair in front of the desk.

'She kept it in here,' Salvör said, opening the bag cautiously and pulling out a day planner with a battered spine. She handed it to Ari Thór.

'Thank you,' he said. 'I trust you won't mind me taking her computer as well. And her phone.'

'Her computer? Her phone?' Salvör stammered. It seemed to take her a moment to process what he was saying. 'I … yes, but I'll get them back, won't I? And the planner too?'

'Of course. We just have to check if there's anything in there that might help us to understand what happened.'

'Do you need anything else?' Salvör asked.

Ari Thór swept his gaze around the room.

'I don't think so. Not for now, anyway.'

He already had a foot out the door into the hall when he realised that Salvör was frozen to the spot in her daughter's room.

'I think I'd better leave you in peace,' he said. 'I'll be in touch as soon as I have any news.'

'OK.' She looked up to meet his eyes and attempted a smile.

'Actually, do you know if there's a password for her laptop? And a code for her phone?' Ari Thór thought he'd better ask.

'A password? Yes. It's just *Unnur4321*. She used the same code for everything. And the code for her phone is *4321*.'

'She told you that?' Ari Thór was surprised.

'Yes,' Salvör replied. 'Like I said, we told each other everything. There were no secrets between us. None at all.'

17

Ari Thór went straight home to pick up his son after leaving Salvör's house. Kristín was keen to get some time to herself and was planning to see some friends in Akureyri – former colleagues from the hospital where she used to work – later that day.

Father and son braved the cold and made their way around the town's various playgrounds, before heading home to warm up. They went upstairs to Stefnir's room to play with his old toys, which didn't seem to capture the boy's interest the way they used to. Still, they had fun lying on the bedroom floor and playing together. After a while, Stefnir began to rub his eyes, so Ari Thór scooped him up, tucked him into bed and read him a story. Before long, they were both fast asleep.

When he opened his eyes after a long nap, Ari Thór woke his son and gave him a bite to eat before letting him go back to sleep.

It was past eight that evening by the time Kristín returned. Ari Thór was sitting at the piano, trying to remember what Ugla had taught him several years earlier before their lessons had come to an abrupt end. Since then, he had tried to teach himself with the help of a few piano books and some sheet music for beginners, but with no great success. He was having trouble concentrating. Every note he played on his out-of-tune piano made him think about Ugla and what a mess he had made of things with her. And now his relationship with Kristín had crumbled to pieces, though to be fair he wasn't the only one to blame. He wouldn't deny there was a temptation to try and patch things up with the mother of his son, but he couldn't help but wonder whether it stemmed more from a sense of duty than a real desire to rekindle the flame.

'So, was he good for you today?' Kristín asked as she walked into the living room.

For a fleeting moment, Ari Thór thought that things were back to normal, just the way they were before. He looked up from the piano and met her gaze.

'We had a great time together. He's fast asleep. I think the fresh sea air is good for him,' he said, suddenly remembering what Gudjón, the artist who had stumbled upon Unnur's body, had said to justify his nocturnal walks around the empty streets.

'Siglufjörður isn't the only place with fresh air,' Kristín replied, with only the slightest hint of bitterness in her voice.

Ari Thór changed the subject. 'How was your day? It must have been nice to see your friends from work again.'

'Oh, they haven't changed a bit. Not that I could see, anyway,' she said. 'They're still working at the hospital, doing the same jobs. Just the same old routine.'

It wasn't clear to Ari Thór if she was being critical of their choices, as she had moved on to bigger and better things, or if she was envious of them and regretted having moved so far away. Why did he find it so difficult to decipher her words and her expression when typically he could read everyone else's like an open book?

'Have you eaten?' he asked.

'Yes, the girls ordered a pizza before I hit the road,' she replied.

Ari Thór's heart sank. He had only had a couple of slices of toast and had been thinking he might order a pizza himself when she got back. That way they could enjoy a quiet evening together and he could get a sense as to whether there was still anything worth salvaging in their relationship.

'Well, I have to admit I'm quite hungry,' he said, hoping that Kristín would suggest calling the pizzeria on Aðalgata, which had been one of their favourite haunts.

Instead, she looked at her watch. 'I imagine the restaurant at the hotel will still be open, won't it?' she said with a smile.

The message was loud and clear. Ari Thór stood up and forced himself to return the smile. 'Of course,' he said. 'I'm not used to living it up like the tourists. What's the plan for tomorrow?'

'Oh, Stefnir and I are quite happy here,' Kristín replied. 'I don't have anything planned, other than just putting my feet up and relaxing. Just come on over whenever you're free. Maybe the two of you could go up to the ski slopes?' she suggested.

Why not, Ari Thór thought. His son was only three, but the earlier he started on skis, the quicker he would learn. And unless something unexpected happened, he didn't see himself leaving Siglufjörður any time in the next few years.

'Yes, the forecast looks quite good,' he replied. 'I should be able to sign him up for a lesson when we get up there.'

'I'll leave that up to you. I suppose you must know everyone by now, even the ski instructors.' Kristín smiled again. 'It'll be nice to have some time all to myself while you two are out having fun together. I'll make you a nice hot chocolate when you get back. How does that sound?'

Again, Ari Thór found it hard to interpret what she was saying. That was the kind of suggestion Kristín would often have made when they were still together as a family – making it seem like she was being considerate towards him but actually pushing him away.

'Sounds great,' he replied warmly, making his way out of the living room and towards the front door.

As he pulled on his parka, he thought he'd give it one last try. 'Actually, do you feel like a glass of red wine?' he asked, looking back into the kitchen. 'I'd be happy to open a bottle. I've still got a couple in the cupboard, and I'll never open them on my own.'

Ari Thór never drank alone and it was rare for him to have visitors in the house.

Again, Kristín looked at her watch. 'I'm tired, Ari. I think I'm just going to head upstairs to bed. I want to lie down next to Stefnir for a little while. I missed him today.'

Ari Thór couldn't argue with that. 'No problem. Maybe another time, then. I'll see if there's anything I feel like at the hotel restaurant.'

❋

Ari Thór made his way back to the hotel, but, mindful of his finances, he had no intention of dining at the restaurant. His inspector's salary was only modest, and the rent he collected from his flat in Reykjavík only just covered the mortgage there. He wasn't in a hurry to sell the place, though. Property values had gone up since he had bought it, and as the years went by, it would become a nice little nest egg for him.

It was a far more tempting prospect to stop at the pizzeria on Aðalgata and pick up something to eat when he got back to his room. The temperature outside had plummeted, and Ari Thór was relieved to be back in the warmth of the hotel. He ate his takeaway pizza in front of a TV documentary about Icelandic history, then he got ready for bed and closed his eyes.

Sleep, however, was a long time coming. Ari Thór couldn't stop thinking about the poor young woman, Unnur. There was something that was bothering him about his conversation with her mother, too. And that wasn't all: he still didn't know what to make of the chilling words that Hávardur had scrawled on the wall in his room at the nursing home.

Ari Thór got out of bed and picked up Unnur's laptop, phone and planner. There was a small desk in his room, beside the TV. He sat there for a while, alone with his thoughts. Soon he found himself craving company – or at least some background noise – so he went down to the hotel bar, taking the laptop and phone with him.

It was a long weekend, but, still, Ari Thór was surprised to see how busy the place was. All the comfy armchairs around the fire were taken, so he had to settle for a table in a quiet corner. He opened the laptop screen cautiously. As he entered the young woman's password, he felt like he was intruding on her privacy. She was essentially a stranger, and Ari Thór couldn't help but wonder what right he had, even as a police officer, to be digging into her personal life. But Unnur's mother was counting on him, and he knew that if there was the slightest chance that a criminal act was at the root of the young woman's death, he had to examine all the potential evidence.

As far as Ari Thór could see, the computer mainly contained essays that Unnur had written for school. There didn't seem to be anything particularly personal in her files. He hesitated for a second, then opened her email program and began browsing through the most recent messages in the inbox. The first two he saw were marked as unread. They had been sent after her death, and were from her high school – as were most of the other messages that scrolled by before his eyes. Ari Thór turned his attention to Unnur's sent messages. These were all polite and courteous, and were written in impeccable Icelandic.

By all appearances, Unnur had been a conscientious young woman who took her studies seriously. Digging a little deeper, Ari Thór came across a few emails she had exchanged with her father, Svavar. He felt a stab of guilt and wondered if it might have been better to obtain permission from both of her parents before prying into Unnur's personal correspondence. The emails to Svavar seemed quite friendly, though, and it looked like they were in regular contact.

Next, Ari Thór saw a series of messages from someone named Sara. He remembered that Salvör had said she was a close friend of Unnur's. He scrolled through the emails the two teenage girls had exchanged. Sara and Unnur were at the same high school. Perhaps they were even in the same class, he thought. As far as he could see, there was no explicit talk about any secrets between them, and nothing about any boyfriends, either.

As the evening went on, the bar became even busier. Most of the customers seemed to be tourists. Ari Thór didn't recognise any faces in the crowd, and he was relieved there was no one here he knew, trying to draw him into conversation. He was happy to sit in silence in the corner of the room and sip the hot chocolate he had ordered.

Ari Thór would have to make it a priority to speak to this Sara and dig beneath the surface of Unnur's life. Although, to be honest, he was starting to doubt there was anything to uncover. But there was nothing wrong with having doubts, he told himself. He just wouldn't let them get in the way of fulfilling his duty to Salvör and finding out what had happened to her daughter. He still didn't know what to do about the creepy message the old man had scrawled on the walls, though. Those words – *she was murdered* – were still sending shivers down his spine.

Ari Thór closed Unnur's laptop and picked up her phone. He entered the code her mother had given him, but nothing jumped out at him. All he saw were a few nondescript apps. And the only conversations in her messaging app were with her parents and her friend Sara. There was nothing at all to suggest that she had been planning to kill herself. Still, he would ask Ögmundur to send the device to police headquarters in Reykjavík for analysis, in case he had missed something.

Ari Thór put the phone down on the table and opened the planner, even more reluctant to infringe on the dead teenager's privacy by reading her handwriting. He turned the pages slowly, one by one. Still he saw nothing that struck him as being out of the ordinary, other than the fact that everything he had examined seemed to be completely devoid of personality. Everything – homework assignments, exam results, appointments – was meticulously organised, both on paper and on Unnur's electronic devices. But there was nothing personal. Nothing at all. And that was odd. It was almost as if someone had fabricated it to make it look like a typical teenager's school planner. Could that actually be the case? Ari Thór had to wonder.

Page by page, he leafed forward in time. Other than homework assignments, Unnur had made a note of barely anything, from the beginning of the school year all the way through to the spring. However, when Ari Thór turned past the page for the day she died, he found that she had written down the dates for an upcoming two-week trip to America to see her father. After that, there was nothing. Unless…

As Ari Thór had suspected, the months covered by the day planner extended past the summer and into the beginning of the following school year. In mid-September, one word stood out from the page in huge letters, followed by a question mark and a heart:

Siglunes? ♥

As if that wasn't intriguing enough, Unnur had then crossed it out, which suggested there had been a change of plan.

Ari Thór had never been to Siglunes, but he had heard of the place. He knew precisely where it was. It was a narrow point of land that extended from the far northern tip of the peninsula separating the fjords of Siglufjörður and Héðinsfjörður. He had sometimes thought about going hiking up there. It was only a few kilometres north of town, but it was on the other shore of the fjord and was extremely difficult to access. It would involve not only a very long walk from the nearest road, but also some scrambling over dangerous rocks and boulders, as the foot of the mountain there was prone to landslides. It would be far easier to get there by boat.

There had once been a small settlement in Siglunes, but that was no longer the case. However, Ari Thór had recently heard that a father and son were renovating an old house up there. He didn't know any more than that. It seemed unlikely that Salvör and her daughter would have any connection to them. What could a teenage girl possibly have been thinking of doing at a remote, abandoned settlement in the middle of September? She had drawn a heart, but Siglunes was hardly a place for a romantic rendezvous. And even if it was, why would it have been planned so far in advance, then cancelled?

Ari Thór would have to ask Salvör if she knew anything about the place. And perhaps he should ask the Reverend

Eggert too. He knew everything about everyone in this town, or so it seemed.

❄

Ari Thór was heading back up to his room when the phone vibrated in his pocket and Ugla's name flashed up on the screen.

Suddenly he felt the need for a breath of fresh air. He found a door in the corridor that opened onto a balcony for hotel guests to use. There was no one else out there, he saw. He stepped outside and closed the door behind him. The air was perfectly still and colder than ice. Ari Thór had never experienced a cold this deep anywhere other than Siglufjörður. It made the ground crunch like snow beneath his feet. He shivered. He hadn't been planning to go outside and wasn't wearing anything over his sweater.

Ari Thór had come to realise that the only way to survive in the northernmost town in Iceland was to embrace all the seasons and resign yourself to your fate. You had to learn to love the bitterly cold winter nights as much as the never-ending summer days, when darkness is nothing but a distant memory and the sun floods the land with warmth and light. And understand how nourishing the cold can be for the body and the soul.

'Hello?' he said, allowing his gaze to get lost in the shadows that enveloped the fjord. There was something mystifying about the lights of the town sinking into the darkness of the cold, still night.

'Hi,' Ugla said. 'I'm sorry to be calling you so late.'

'Oh, it's no problem at all,' Ari Thór replied. 'I was still awake. I had work to do.'

'Were you working on the case?' she asked. 'Have you been looking into Hávardur and his background?'

'No, I'm looking at other aspects of the girl's death at the moment,' Ari Thór replied, as it dawned on him that Ugla might be suggesting the subjects of the message on the wall and the fateful fall were one and the same.

'Ah, OK. I just wanted to tell you something, in the strictest confidence, of course…' Ugla said, with a hint of reluctance – or fear – in her voice.

'I'm listening,' Ari Thór replied. 'Is everything all right?'

She hesitated. 'Yes, yes. It's just that I spoke to Hersir earlier … Well, he called me, to be precise. He wasn't happy.'

'What do you mean, he wasn't happy?'

'That I'd spoken to you.'

She fell silent for a moment before adding: 'Actually, that's an understatement. He flew into a blind rage.'

'Really?' Ari Thór was both intrigued and concerned.

'Yes, I … I think I'm lucky he didn't fire me. He told me I'd made a grave mistake.'

'How so?'

'He said I shouldn't be running off and telling tales to the police. Not for something as trivial as that. What I did was a breach of confidentiality, and it was a very serious matter, he said. And he said he'd thought he could trust me…'

'And I imagine he's not expecting you to be telling me all this now?'

'No, absolutely not. I don't think he knows that we … that we're friends, Ari Thór.'

The last thing she said left Ari Thór feeling a bit puzzled. They hadn't spoken in years, and now Ugla was referring to him as a friend. Her words took him by surprise at first, but then he had to admit he found it flattering that she thought of him that way.

'Well, that's certainly a strange way to react,' he said. 'Don't worry, I'll keep this to myself. You did the right thing by telling me, Ugla. It would be perfectly normal for anyone who saw what you saw to contact the police.'

'I hope you're right,' she replied. 'I think he might just be concerned about the consequences of something like this for his care home. I know things weren't easy in the beginning, and he and his wife Rósa have put everything they own into making a go of the place. Buying the building from the municipality and doing all the renovation work ... I dread to think how much that must have cost. I do know that for the care home to be viable, they needed to get regulatory approval from the government to provide medical services. As well as granting them a permit, approval would open the door for funding down the line, you see.'

'And they had trouble with that?' Ari Thór asked.

'It kept getting tied up in red tape. The authorities kept saying the approval was in the works, but the fact of the matter is, the place had to open to residents sooner or later and it wouldn't stay afloat without funding.'

'And how are things going now?'

'Better, I think. Hersir hasn't seemed as stressed lately. The bank has stopped hassling him, and apparently there's some funding coming through the pipes in time for next winter. So, the worst has passed. I like Hersir and Rósa, and I like my job. I can see myself having a future there, and I have no desire to leave Siglufjörður, except if I decide to go back to college for a while.'

Ari Thór didn't say anything. He was still dubious about the doctor's reaction, and was mulling it over in his mind.

'What about you?' Ugla suddenly asked.

'Me?'

'Do you ever think about leaving Sigló?'

He noticed that she used the locals' nickname for the town, one that he'd never used himself, but was starting to feel an inclination to. It had been a long time since anyone had asked Ari Thór the question.

Obviously, he and Kristín had discussed their future here when they were still together, but since she had moved away, it had not really been any of her concern whether he stayed or left, even though they had shared custody of Stefnir.

Ari Thór had also talked a lot with Tómas about how the future might involve Reykjavík – both before his old boss ended up moving away himself to live in the capital, and for a while afterwards too. Over time, their working relationship had developed into a friendship, and in spite of the age gap between them they had essentially become each other's confidant. To Ari Thór's regret, they seemed to have fallen out of touch lately.

'Sometimes, but not any time soon,' Ari Thór replied, after an awkward silence.

By now, he felt a strong sense of connection to Siglufjörður. Something was keeping him here, but he couldn't quite put his finger on what. It was almost as if the place didn't want him to leave. It had never crossed his mind that he might end up spending the rest of his life in this small town, but he had to admit he had grown to love the isolation and tranquillity of the place.

'Well anyway, keep it to yourself, what I told you, all right?' Ugla urged.

'No worries,' Ari Thór replied, though he still had every intention of paying Hersir another visit.

'I think I'm going to go to bed now,' Ugla said. 'Sorry again for bothering you.'

'Oh, you didn't bother me at all,' he reassured her.

'Maybe we'll see each other this weekend, then,' she added. 'I'm not going anywhere either. I have to work too.'

Ari Thór wondered if she was trying to tell him something. Maybe this was a sign that it was time for them to give things another go. But he didn't want to get his hopes up.

'Yes, I'm sure we will,' he replied, before wishing her good night and ending the call.

The north wind was starting to pick up. It was time for him to seek peace beneath the covers and let the night take its course.

SATURDAY

18

The next morning, Ari Thór had something of a rude awakening. He hadn't intended to stay in bed particularly late, even though it was the weekend, but he was still in a deep sleep when the sound of his ringing phone jolted him awake, making him curse out loud.

He blinked his eyes open to see the name on the screen: *Salvör*. He had given Unnur's mother his mobile number when he left her house the previous day, just in case. And right now, he bitterly regretted having done so.

He let the phone ring, got out of bed and pulled the thick curtains from the window. It was past nine o'clock already. Outside, the snow was coming down thick and fast, like it always seemed to do in Siglufjörður. Snow as heavy as this was rare in the south of the country, except perhaps in Ari Thór's childhood memories, as unreliable as those probably were. As he remembered, there had always been something special about the Saturday before Easter.

His parents had not been devout, but in their house, Good Friday was a day to be religiously observed. For a young boy, that day had seemed interminable, and so the Saturday had always felt like a liberation for the young Ari Thór. Often, on that Saturday night, their little family would go out for hamburgers rather than cook dinner at home. Perhaps he could twist Kristín's arm and let him take her and

Stefnir out to a restaurant on Aðalgata tonight. Wouldn't it be nice, he thought, to have some semblance of a normal family life, like he had always dreamed of, if only for a fleeting moment?

He grabbed his phone from the bedside table and returned Salvör's call. She hadn't left a voicemail message.

'Hello?' she replied, hesitantly. 'Is that you, Ari Thór? I hope I didn't disturb you.'

'Not at all,' he replied, rubbing his eyes.

'I was calling to tell you that Svavar, Unnur's father, arrived last night. He'd like to speak with you, if that's possible. I know it's the weekend, and—'

'It's no trouble,' Ari Thór reassured her.

'Thank you so much,' Salvör sighed wearily. 'Have … have there been any new developments?'

'No, I'm afraid not.'

Ari Thór resisted the temptation to tell her that, even though he still had a few leads to follow up, nothing was likely to change. That in all probability, the police would not find an explanation for her daughter's actions, and they would not find anyone to point the finger at.

'That's what I suspected.' Salvör released a long sigh.

Ari Thór was about to hang up when something suddenly occurred to him. 'Can I ask you a question, Salvör?'

'Yes, of course.'

'Does the word or name "Siglunes" mean anything to you?'

'Siglunes?' Salvör sounded as if she had been caught off guard.

'Yes, you know—'

'I know it's the name of a place, and I know where it is, but I've never been,' she interjected. 'It's not an easy place to get to, and I'm not much of a hiker. Why … why do you ask?'

Ari Thór hesitated. Should he tell her what he had seen, and risk planting a seed of hope that this poor grieving woman might find answers to the awful questions that must be tormenting her day and night?

He decided to bite the bullet. 'Your daughter wrote that word in her day planner,' he said, wishing he had waited until he was face to face with Salvör so he could see her reaction.

'How so? What's that supposed to mean?'

'I don't know, but it jumped off the page at me,' Ari Thór replied. 'It was so out of keeping with everything else. The only other things she wrote in there were to do with school and homework.'

'I don't understand,' Salvör said. 'She never went to Siglunes, not…' Her words faded to a whisper. 'Not to my knowledge.'

'Do you know anyone there?' Ari Thór asked.

A moment of silence hung in the air before Salvör replied: 'In a way. There's a man and his son working on a house up there. They're distant cousins of mine … but I don't actually know them.'

'Do you think Unnur might have known them, though?'

'I doubt it.'

Salvör's words were confident, but Ari Thór thought he could hear some uncertainty in her voice.

Unnur's brutal death must have caused her mother to question everything she thought she knew about her daughter. What kind of secret must she have been hiding? What was so terrible that it would drive her to…

'Maybe it doesn't mean anything at all. Let's not dwell on it.' Ari Thór tried to sound reassuring. But he was sure that simple word the teenage girl had written – and crossed out – must mean something. And he was determined to get to the bottom of the mystery.

'But if anything does come to mind…' he prompted.

'I really can't see what she would have been doing there,' Salvör said, after a brief pause. 'She never talked to me about going up there. She never talked about Siglunes at all. She wrote it in her planner, you said?'

'Yes,' Ari Thór said.

'What was the date?'

'It was in September. I don't recall the exact date.'

'She's … she was so meticulous and organised. If she made a note of something in her planner, that means she was intending to follow through with it. But…'

Ari Thór filled the silence. 'Why would she go to Siglunes in September? For a hike, perhaps? Or a weekend away camping?'

'No, that really wasn't her sort of thing.' Her voice was so weak, it was hanging by a thread.

Ari Thór realised how difficult it must be for Salvör to talk about this, and decided to change the subject.

'What about Unnur's father? Where can I find him?'

'Svavar's staying at the hotel on the waterfront,' she replied.

'Oh, that's handy,' Ari Thór replied. 'That's where I am right now, as it happens. It's a long story. If you give me his mobile number, I'll get in touch with him.'

19

The first thing that struck Ari Thór as he sat down at the breakfast table in the hotel restaurant, across from Svavar, was how different the man seemed from his ex-wife. Salvör had been visibly shaken or vocally distraught every time Ari Thór had seen or spoken to her, and that was perfectly understandable, given the horrific circumstances. She was in shock. By contrast, Svavar looked to be holding his grief inside himself.

The man's plate was piled high, as if he had travelled all the way across the ocean on an empty stomach and was making up for lost time by sampling everything the breakfast buffet had to offer.

Ari Thór introduced himself and expressed his condolences. Svavar tucked in to his breakfast and waited for what seemed like an eternity to pass before eventually giving Ari Thór the time of day. He looked up from his plate and took a swig of coffee, then opened his mouth to unleash his arrogance.

'So you're the man who's trying to find out what happened to my daughter?'

'Yes, I—'

Svavar didn't let him get another word in. 'Aren't you a bit young to shoulder the responsibility for this level of investigation?' he snapped, frowning down his nose at Ari Thór.

Ari Thór didn't let Svavar's attitude throw him off. He knew the poor man must be racked with anguish, even though he wasn't showing it.

'I am Inspector Ari Thór Arason,' he reminded the man gently. 'I was the first person to be notified about your daughter's death. I know this must be a hard time for you. I can assure you, we're doing everything we can to find out what happened to Unnur. However, to be perfectly honest with you, I'm not convinced that this investigation will tell us anything we don't already know.'

'You must be joking,' Svavar scoffed. 'There's definitely something fishy here. My Unnur would never have thrown herself off a balcony, do you understand that? It's completely unthinkable. Someone else is to blame, I know it. If you don't think you can find out who that person is, then you're not cut out for your job. And we're going to have to look elsewhere for answers.'

Ari Thór kept his cool. 'I'm very sorry for what happened to your daughter, Svavar. Do you have any reason to believe that someone could have meant her any harm?'

'I just know that she would never have killed herself. She was a tower of strength, that girl. There was nothing she couldn't cope with, and she got that from me,' Svavar said gravely.

'Do you think someone could have...?' Ari Thór ventured.

'I don't know anything about her life here, all right? I don't know who she was friends with and who she was seeing. It's your job to find that out.'

'What *do* you know about your daughter's life, if you don't mind me asking?'

That seemed to shake Svavar's self-assurance and give him some pause for thought. He glared at Ari Thór, as if to say: *How dare you?* Then he spoke, weighing every word carefully.

'I do take an interest, of course, but my ex-wife has done everything she can to keep my daughter and me apart.'

'Was it a difficult divorce?'

'I'd rather not go into details. Things didn't exactly end well between us. And nothing has really improved since then. I came here for Unnur. Salvör is not my concern anymore.'

'I understand you live in Boston,' Ari Thór said.

'Yeah.' Svavar didn't elaborate.

'What do you do over there?'

'I … I'm out of work at the moment. My wife's a doctor, so we're doing all right. I don't actually have a work permit. I haven't got around to applying.'

'And before you went over there, you were a sailor?' Ari Thór continued.

'It sounds like you already know the answer to all your questions.'

Ari Thór didn't reply, waiting instead for Svavar to fill the silence.

'Yes, I was a ship's captain for many years,' he eventually said. 'That kind of work is exhausting. It really takes its toll on you in the end. I was always away from home. And that wasn't exactly a recipe for a happy family life.'

'If I say "Siglunes", does that mean anything to you?'

'Siglunes? Yes, but I've never been. People used to go shark hunting from there, long ago. But I never did. Why do you ask?'

'Unnur wrote the name of the place in her diary,' Ari Thór told him.

'She had a diary?' Unnur's father sounded surprised.

'Well, it was more of a day planner, something she used to keep track of her school work,' Ari Thór admitted. 'That's why the name jumped out at me, because it wasn't in keeping with anything else she'd written.'

For now, he decided to keep to himself the fact that the man's teenage daughter had drawn a heart beside the name.

Svavar planted his elbows on the table and leaned across it, creasing his eyes and asserting his authority once more. 'You have to get to the bottom of this, Ari Thór. I believe someone killed my daughter, and it's your job to find out who.'

Ari Thór wasn't quite sure how to react. He was tempted to bow down and promise the man he would do everything he could, but before he could open his mouth, Svavar made his point even more strongly.

'I'll be staying here until this is all settled. And mark my words, I won't stand for any amateur incompetence.'

The man was clearly very serious. He had no work to draw him back to the United States, so he could linger as long as he wanted in Iceland.

Ari Thór stood up and thanked Svavar for his time. Just to be safe, he resolved to ask Ögmundur to check that the man had just arrived back in the country, as he claimed, and to eliminate any possibility that he might have already been in Siglufjörður at the time of his daughter's death.

And then something else crossed his mind. *I'd rather not say anything*, Svavar had said, when Ari Thór had steered the conversation towards Salvör. So it had been a difficult divorce, he mused. Was there something unusual about his ex-wife's behaviour that he would rather not bring up? Was there any possibility that she had something to hide as far as her daughter's death was concerned?

Ari Thór had a hard time imagining that, but once the seed of doubt was planted, there was no getting rid of it.

20

'Ah, Ari Thór! To what do I owe the pleasure?'

As usual, the Reverend Eggert appeared to be in the lightest of moods. He was a cheerful man, who had filled part of the void that had been left in Ari Thór's life when Tómas moved away. He was someone Ari Thór could turn to in any situation, someone good for the soul in more ways than one.

The Reverend Eggert had proven himself invaluable a few years earlier, when Ari Thór had been investigating a suspicious death in Héðinsfjördur with a mysterious connection to the past. Now the young inspector needed his friend's assistance in a case that was just as tragic and far more current.

Ari Thór was now sitting in his hotel room, talking to the reverend on the phone.

'I'm sorry to bother you,' he said. 'I know you must be busy preparing for the Easter service in church tomorrow.'

'Oh, don't worry, that's all been ready for a while,' Reverend Eggert replied. 'I don't like to leave things to the last minute. Now, a little bird told me you were living it up at the hotel, is that right?'

As always, news travelled fast in this small town.

'Kristín and my son are here for the weekend, and I've given them the house to themselves,' he explained. 'I thought it might be a bit awkward if we were all under the same roof.'

'It'll all come out in the wash, don't you worry. I know there are some little bumps for you to iron out, but you'll be fine.'

Ari Thór found his friend's optimism endearing, but felt like he had to say something, if only to avoid disillusioning him later on.

'Well, we haven't really talked about where we're at,' he admitted. 'But obviously, there's no harm in hope.'

'If only for your son's sake,' Reverend Eggert replied. 'How old is he now?'

'He's three already.'

'Ah yes, of course. Well, I'm sure you'll both do the best you can.'

'Actually, there was something I wanted to ask you…'

'I'm all ears, Ari Thór.'

'It's about the young woman who died. I wanted to know if she had any connection to Siglunes. Does that ring a bell? I imagine the history of the place holds no secrets for a man like you.'

'The history of Siglunes? My dear Ari Thór, I've written page upon page about that magical place stretching out into the fjord.'

Reverend Eggert paused for a moment as a thought seeped into his mind.

'How would you like to join me for a little jaunt up there? It's not far by boat. We'll be there in no time.'

Ari Thór knew that the previous summer Reverend Eggert had clubbed together with a few friends to buy a small powerboat. He had often seen them motoring up and down the fjord.

'Er … yes, of course. But is it safe to go on the water at this time of year?'

'Oh, the weather's glorious today. Not a breath of wind. The water looks as calm as a millpond. I see no reason not to, if you're up for a little adventure. Just bring a good coat to keep the chill off.'

Ari Thór had promised to meet up with Kristín and Stefnir that morning, but he couldn't pass up an opportunity like this.

'How long will it take?' he asked.

'Oh, it's just a stone's throw away. We'll be there in ten, fifteen minutes at most, then it's up to you how long you want to stay once we make land. The two fellows who've moved up there are a joy to talk to.'

'You know what? I'm not sure there's any real reason to go.'

Ari Thór was starting to have second thoughts about the idea. He was certainly interested in visiting the place, but he had no desire whatsoever to waste any more of his precious weekend. The chances that the teenager's death was actually linked to Siglunes were slim at best, he reasoned.

'Don't be silly, Ari Thór. I'd love to make myself useful. Can you be ready in half an hour? I'm always happy to take the boat out on the water.'

Well, it couldn't hurt to head out there and have a look, Ari Thór thought. 'Half an hour? That's doable. I'll meet you at the harbour.'

'Don't forget, you'll want to dress up warm.'

'Of course.'

Ari Thór figured he had just enough time to dash home and grab a thicker sweater.

When he got there, Stefnir and Kristín were up and dressed. He explained that he was just stopping by and apologised that he wouldn't be able to look after Stefnir until an hour or so later than they had arranged. To his surprise, that didn't seem to bother Kristín in the slightest. He couldn't help but think that her indifference to these last-minute changes of plan – which were tantamount to him prioritising work over family – were another sign that their relationship was beyond repair.

Reverend Eggert was waiting on the wharf when Ari Thór got there.

'It's a pleasure to see you, my dear Ari Thór!' he exclaimed. 'How did you know I was looking for a good reason to take the boat out on the water? If you hadn't called, I would probably have just stayed at home in the warm. The older we get, the more we um and ah and end up trapped in the same old routine. So when you called, it was like a gift from the heavens. There she is, our pride and joy.'

He pointed to a rather aggressive-looking, rigid-hulled inflatable boat equipped with a large outboard motor. Ari Thór had never learned how to sail or to drive a motorboat, but it wasn't for lack of interest. He had always been fascinated by the ocean and felt drawn to it as if he had saltwater running through his veins. He didn't have to look very far to find a family connection to the water. There had been quite a few sailors on his mother's side. Perhaps some of them had even gone shark hunting around Siglunes, he thought.

'Make yourself comfortable and put this on,' Reverend Eggert said, handing him a day-glow orange life vest. 'There are strict regulations for bringing passengers aboard. And believe me, chins would be wagging if anyone saw a servant of the man upstairs flouting the rules!' he added, with a wicked glint in his eye.

Reverend Eggert started the outboard motor and eased the boat away from the dock, into the fjord. The cold grew more and more biting as they accelerated away from the shore. The water was calm at first, but became choppier as they left the town in their wake.

The reverend took it upon himself to start telling all kinds of stories about the area as they skimmed over the water's surface towards Siglunes, but it was hard for Ari Thór to hear over the roaring of the outboard motor and the thudding of the hull against the chop. Truth be told, he was only listening with half an ear. He was too busy admiring the scenery and looking ahead. Slowly but surely, the outlines of the former settlement were emerging on the narrow strip of land he could see jutting out into the mouth of the fjord.

Ari Thór loved living up here, in Siglufjörður. Times like these, when the locals seemed to think of him as one of their own, made Ari Thór really feel at home. It occurred to him that since he had been made inspector, people had stopped seeing him as an outsider. Perhaps it was because he had survived enough northern winters for them to consider him one of their own, or maybe they saw his appointment to a position with greater responsibility as a commitment to the community – a sign that he planned to stick around.

When the Reverend Eggert stopped talking for a moment, Ari Thór seized the opportunity to get up and sit right at the front of the boat. As they approached Siglunes, a number of house-shaped silhouettes slowly came into view. The wind whipped at his face, but Ari Thór kept looking straight ahead.

'As I'm sure you can imagine, there's no dock on the shore here,' Reverend Eggert called to him from the helm. 'So long as it's calm enough when we get there, we'll just run the boat up on the shore. We shouldn't have much to worry about today,' he added.

Ari Thór turned to look at the reverend. 'So these waters can be dangerous, then?' he asked.

'Oh, they certainly can be. I've heard plenty of stories of shipwrecks around here. One I remember very well: six men died at sea and one of them was too tall for his coffin. Apparently they had to cut his feet off so he'd fit. You can just imagine the tales they told about that in the fishermen's huts. People used to say they'd seen the ghost of the man crawling around with stumps for ankles.'

The thought of that gave Ari Thór chills. He decided to change the subject.

'Are you sure the man and his son are here right now?' he asked, moving closer to make sure his friend could hear him.

'I'm certain they are. I can see their boat pulled up on the shore, and I don't see what might have possessed them to leave the place on foot at this time of year, unless there was an emergency.'

Ari Thór turned back to look at the houses on the strip of land ahead. They weren't far away now. It would be a stretch of the imagination to call what was left of Siglunes a village. The handful of dilapidated structures were barely enough to qualify the place as a hamlet. It seemed strange to see signs of civilisation in such a bleak, inhospitable setting. It occurred to Ari Thór that no one would live in a place like this unless they had no other choice – or considered it an adventure just to survive out here, in extreme isolation.

'Let's go ashore here, where the beach is sandy,' Reverend Eggert said. 'The conditions are easy enough right now.'

He manoeuvred the boat far more ably than Ari Thór would have thought, accelerating hard towards the shore, then killing the engine and tilting the outboard motor forward just in time so that it wouldn't hit the ground. The momentum carried the boat up onto the beach easily, and they stepped out onto the sand without getting their feet wet.

They didn't have to look very far to find the sole residents of Siglunes: no sooner had they stepped off the boat than two men emerged from a house and started walking towards them.

'Hello there!' Reverend Eggert called. He obviously didn't need to introduce himself.

The older of the two, a stocky, heavily balding man who looked to be well into his sixties, nodded in greeting before turning and extending a hand to Ari Thór. He was wearing a grubby red lumberjack shirt and clearly hadn't shaved for days. What remained of the hair on his head hung long and unkempt around his collar.

'Hello,' he said with a surprisingly warm smile. 'My name's Thorleifur.'

The younger of the two men stepped forward in turn and introduced himself.

'I'm Thorleifur too.'

'He's my son,' the older man explained, looking Ari Thór in the eye. 'Thorleifur and Thorleifur, father and son at your service.'

'Inspector Ari Thór Arason.'

'We know who you are,' Thorleifur senior replied. 'This must be your first time visiting this part of your jurisdiction, I imagine.'

Ari Thór nodded, though he wasn't sure whether his authority actually extended to Siglunes.

'I'm not surprised. It's not as if there's much crime this far from town. There's not much excitement here. Never has been, as far as I can recall.'

In different circumstances, those words might have been construed as critical, but in that moment, on the tranquil, remote beach in Siglunes, they could only be words of praise. Here, monotony was a virtue. As he stood on the sand, Ari Thór felt a sense of stillness rising within him. It had to be something to do with the silence, and being so close to nature, he thought.

'Welcome to the place we call home,' Thorleifur senior continued.

He pointed to the house he and his son had emerged from a moment earlier. Just a few steps away, it was a two-storey building with dormer windows in the attic – not unlike the house on Aðalgata where Unnur's body had been found, Ari Thór thought. The siding was stone-grey and in need of a lick of paint. If it wasn't for the two huge, new-looking windows overlooking the fjord on each floor, it would have been easy to think the place was abandoned.

'Please, do come in.' Thorleifur senior ushered Ari Thór and Reverend Eggert through the front door. 'We weren't exactly expecting visitors, but my son just got back from town, so we have a few things in the cupboard. We can at least pretend to be decent hosts. Well, we have coffee, at any rate,' he joked.

The renovation work was further along inside the house.

'We're going to redo the siding this summer,' Thorleifur senior continued. 'We've made good progress on the interior this winter. No one's lived out here in the cold and dark for years, but we've managed to survive so far.'

'Please make yourselves comfortable,' Thorleifur junior said. 'I'll make the coffee. Will you both have some?'

'I wouldn't mind some milk in mine, if you have any,' Reverend Eggert replied.

'Do you have any tea?' Ari Thór asked.

The younger man looked at him as if he'd never heard of the stuff.

'Black coffee will be fine,' Ari Thór hastened to add, deciding he would rather make do than go without. Though his tastes had broadened in recent years, he still preferred tea.

'So, what brings you here?' Thorleifur senior asked, sitting down at an antique wooden table in the living room and motioning for them to join him. The chairs and stools were all mismatched.

Ari Thór wanted to wait until the man's son was in the room before he got down to the crux of the matter, so instead of answering his question, he posed one himself.

'If you don't mind me asking, what was it that drew you to Siglunes?' he said. 'It looks like it's taken a lot of work to make this old house liveable.'

The older man nodded. 'We've been here since last summer. The house has been in the family for generations, but no one had lived here for many years, and it had started to go to ruin, like all the other abandoned places here. But we've always loved this place. It has a real sentimental value for us. So much of our family history happened within these four walls. My son and I had often talked about doing the place up, and at first we thought we'd come up a few weekends every summer and do things gradually, take things one step at a time, you know ... But then circumstances changed, so we had to kick into gear faster than we were planning to. I'm not saying we're going to make this our forever home, but we'll stay until the autumn at least. We should have finished all the work by then. Maybe we'll open our doors to tourists eventually, so they can get a sense of the wilderness out here. It looks like business is booming in town these days, with that fancy hotel and all those new restaurants popping up.'

'Ah yes, it would be a lovely spot for a bed and breakfast, or perhaps an artist's retreat,' Reverend Eggert suggested.

'Now there's an idea,' Thorleifur senior replied.

'You said that circumstances had changed,' Ari Thór interrupted. 'What happened?'

For a moment, Thorleifur didn't say anything. His son was still in the kitchen.

After a few seconds, he broke the silence. 'It's not a secret.

Most people will have heard what happened. My wife died last year, very suddenly.'

'My condolences,' Ari Thór replied.

'Thank you. To be honest, my son's been in a spot of bother too. He was in prison for…'

Thorleifur didn't get to finish his sentence, as his son now emerged from the kitchen carrying two mugs of coffee for their guests.

'An absolute injustice, if you ask me,' he snorted, picking up the story as if this wasn't the first time he had had to explain himself. His words were tinged with regret and bitterness. 'I was working in a bank before the crisis happened. I had been for years. I was just an average employee. I kept my head down and did my job, but I found myself mixed up in one of the investigations into who was responsible for the crash. I had to serve a prison sentence for a few months. It was too much for my wife, and she left me.'

'So anyway,' Thorleifur senior continued, 'my son and I both found ourselves alone and at a loss as to what to do with ourselves. I'm a contractor by trade, but work had been drying up for a while, so there was nothing to stop us from making this dream of ours a reality. And we had quite a bit of money saved up, so we could afford to do it. You could say we decided to make the best of the situation.'

Ari Thór nodded.

'But that's enough about our troubles,' Thorleifur senior said. 'I imagine this isn't just a social call?'

'It's nothing that should concern you directly,' Ari Thór reassured him. 'Reverend Eggert kindly offered to bring me out here in his boat, because the name Siglunes has cropped up as part of a current investigation. To be honest, I've always been curious to see the place too. It's so close to Siglufjörður, but at the same time it seems so far away.'

'So … how is Siglunes connected to your investigation, exactly?' Thorleifur junior asked.

Ari Thór thought he could detect a slight tremor in the young man's voice. Did he have something to hide? Or was this just wariness stemming from his past brush with the law?

'It's a matter concerning a young woman who was found dead early on Thursday morning.'

'Oh, really?' Thorleifur senior exclaimed, turning to Ari Thór and raising an eyebrow. 'We don't know the girl at all.'

'I understand you were related,' Ari Thór replied. He was surprised they had even heard the news.

'Well, technically, yes, but only on paper. I'm sure you'll find everyone in Siglufjörður shares some sort of bloodline. But we've never had any contact with her.'

'What about her mother?'

Thorleifur senior shook his head and looked at his son. 'No, not with her, either,' he said.

'Is it possible that the girl came over here during the winter, or maybe that she was planning to visit Siglunes in the summer or the autumn?'

Father and son exchanged a glance, then Thorleifur senior replied: 'We've been here all winter. At least one of us has been at the house the whole time. It's not an easy place to get into or out of in the cold and the dark, you know. I can't picture myself trying to hike over the mountain and trudge my way through the snow and ice, and I won't take the boat out in all weathers either. Same goes for anyone else who wants to come exploring up here. Obviously, I can't tell you if that poor girl or anyone in her family had any plans to come here. No one's said anything to us, anyway. We don't own the whole place, you know, just the house and a little plot of land. People are free to come and go as they please anywhere else on the point.'

He paused as if to catch his breath, then added: 'Of course, people do just show up out of the blue sometimes.'

The remark seemed to leave a sour taste in the man's mouth, and Ari Thór couldn't help but feel that it was directed at him and Reverend Eggert.

'Do you see a lot of tourists, then?' the reverend asked.

'In the summer, yes. They like to come and camp when the weather's nice. The footpath from Siglufjörður is quite popular with hikers, and the terrain isn't that difficult in the right season. To be honest, my son and I are actually looking forward to the summer. It'll do us good to have some company, and it'll be nice for there to be a bit more life around the place. And with a bit of luck, the house should look more presentable by then.'

'What's the path like in the autumn?' Ari Thór asked.

The older man seemed surprised by the question. 'Well, like I said, it's not that tricky to negotiate. A lot of the time, it's passable even up until the beginning of winter. It all depends on the weather, of course.'

'Are you aware of anything that might be happening here in September this year?'

'In September? What do you mean?'

'Some sort of event, perhaps?' Ari Thór pressed.

Thorleifur senior shrugged and smiled. 'I'm not sure what you're getting at. We don't have any parties planned, if that's what you're wondering. Our hands are full enough with the work on the house.'

'Right then,' said Reverend Eggert, making a move to get up from his chair. 'Let's not bother these gentlemen all day, shall we, Ari Thór?'

'Actually, there's just one more thing,' said Ari Thór, taking a sip of his coffee.

He saw no reason why they should be in a hurry. The father and son didn't get many visitors at this time of year, he presumed, so they probably appreciated the company. That said, he had promised Kristín that he wouldn't be too long.

He directed his question at Thorleifur junior: 'Your father said you just got back from town. I imagine he meant Siglufjörður?'

'That's right,' the younger man replied, hesitantly.

'How long were you gone?'

'How long?'

Ari Thór smiled and waited for the man to reply. The question was clear enough.

'I ... er, I went in on Wednesday and I came back yesterday. I was staying with a friend. I had a few errands to run, and it's nice to get away from here once in a while. To see people, you know, and have a beer or two in a bar...' He was speaking quickly and sounded almost too sure of himself. 'Why do you ask?' he added.

'As it happens, the young woman – Unnur – died two days ago, in the early hours of Thursday morning. And you've just told me you were in Siglufjörður at that time, have you not?'

Thorleifur junior and senior looked dumbfounded. Ari Thór hadn't come here to make enemies. But he hadn't come to make friends either.

The son jumped to his feet angrily, ignoring his father's efforts to get him to calm down.

'Who do you think you are?' he hissed. 'You have the cheek to turn up unannounced and breeze into our house and accuse me of ... of...'

'Murder?' Ari Thór suggested. 'I said nothing of the sort.'

The younger man lost any composure he still had. 'No, that's not what I meant, but … I just don't understand why you decided to come out here if…'

This was Ari Thór's cue to stand up and make an exit.

'Thank you very much for your time,' he said, as Reverend Eggert followed his lead. 'And thank you for the coffee. We can't stay and finish it, unfortunately. We weren't planning to stay too long, you see. It's going to be a busy day, by the looks of it.'

Thorleifur senior nodded, stood up and shook his guests by the hand.

'It was a pleasure,' he said. 'You'll have to come back another time, in more pleasant circumstances. Siglunes is stunning in the summertime, as I'm sure you can imagine.'

The man bid them farewell with a casual air, but the thinly veiled concern on his face did not escape Ari Thór's notice.

21

On his return from Siglunes, Ari had taken little Stefnir up to the ski slopes for the afternoon, as Kristín had suggested, while she put her feet up for a while at the house on Eyrargata.

The skiing had been an adventure for both of them. Rather than booking a private lesson just for his son, Ari Thór had decided to join him, thinking it would be a good bonding experience. Stefnir had squealed with delight to be sliding on skis in the snow. Their instructor, a young woman from Siglufjörður, had been especially patient with her two absolute novice skiers.

The mountain was a stunning place to be in the winter sun. The weather had stayed fine all day, and neither the snow nor the wind had got in the way of their fun. After his encounter with Svavar at the hotel, the boat trip to Siglunes that morning and the high spirits on the ski slopes that afternoon, Ari Thór was looking forward to a relaxing evening. He and Stefnir were driving back into town, on their way to meet Kristín at the hotel bar for a hot chocolate, when Ögmundur called.

Ari Thór was reluctant to answer the phone. He sighed, turning his gaze to the fjord, which was shimmering in the light of the setting sun. Then he took a deep breath, savouring the feeling of peace and quiet for one more second before he accepted the call. He had instructed his second-in-command only to bother him if it was a matter of absolute necessity.

Ögmundur got straight to the point. 'Ari Thór, there's a girl here who wants to talk to you.'

'A girl?' Ari Thór didn't see how this could possibly be urgent.

'She says her name's Jenný. That's all I know.'

'Can't this wait? I'm busy. Just take her statement,' Ari Thór replied, not bothering to hide the frustration in his voice.

'She's insisting on talking to you. And I'm not really up to speed with the Unnur investigation,' Ögmundur protested.

Ari Thór sighed. 'And she told you it had to do with that case, I presume?'

'She didn't have to. It's obvious. It's not like we're investigating anything else right now, is it?' Ögmundur quipped, probably not realising how disrespectful that sounded.

'Can't you just take care of it, Ögmundur? I'm in the car with my son at the moment.'

'Listen, you're the one she wants to speak to. Her old man knows you, apparently, and it's a sensitive matter. That's all she's told me,' he insisted.

❄

Once they were back in town, Ari Thór left Stefnir with Kristín, then walked over to the police station. There he found a teenage girl sitting at Ögmundur's desk, her head in her hands.

Usually, members of the public were not allowed past the reception area, unless they were under arrest. Ögmundur had clearly bent the rules for her. It wasn't the first time he'd done that sort of thing. But seeing the state the young woman was in, Ari Thór had to admit he would probably have done the same.

'Jenný?' he asked gently, turning to her after nodding at Ögmundur in greeting.

She gave a start and jerked her head upright. Her eyes were filled with tears.

'Why don't we go into my office?' Ari Thór suggested, taking off his parka.

She stood up and followed him.

'Apparently I know your father,' he said to break the ice, once they were both seated.

'Yes, he works at the library. You must have crossed paths with him here and there. His name's Bolli.'

Ari Thór nodded. The name sounded familiar, even though he couldn't quite place the man.

'He always speaks highly of you, so I wanted to talk directly to you, if that's all right.'

'Of course,' Ari Thór replied patiently.

He waited to hear what Jenný had to say. When she made no effort to fill the silence, he prompted her.

'Is this about Unnur? Did you know her?'

She nodded. 'We were friends, in a way…'

'What do you mean, "in a way"?'

'Unnur wasn't very sociable. She wasn't the type to hang out with lots of friends, I mean. But we got on quite well, and we were in the same class…' She seemed reluctant to continue.

'She was friends with a girl named Sara, wasn't she?' Ari Thór asked, remembering the emails he had read.

'Yes, Sara was probably her best friend, but … they weren't even that close either. Their mums were friends, so that kind of obligated Sara and Unnur to be friends too. They would help each other out at school and things, but…' She left the words hanging.

'What kind of girl was she? Can you describe her to me?' Ari Thór asked.

'What do you mean?' Jený put her head in her hands again and mumbled the rest of her answer. 'She was as quiet as a mouse. She would never get herself into any kind of trouble. She was far too naive and innocent to be led astray.'

Ari Thór was intrigued by Jený's choice of words. He waited patiently for her to continue, not wanting to pressure her in any way. She seemed distraught enough as it was.

'I ... I walked down Aðalgata earlier...' she stammered after a moment of silence. 'I went there, you know ... to see where she fell. I was standing in front of the building when I saw ... I saw...'

She sprang up from her chair and, despite an obvious effort to control her emotions, burst into tears.

'There was no need for her to die,' she eventually said, with a sigh.

'What did you see?' Ari Thór asked, standing up too.

Jený shook her head, wiped her eyes and looked away. 'Nothing, I'm sorry. It's nothing ... I shouldn't have come.'

With these words, she turned and ran towards the exit. Ari Thór grabbed his parka and followed her, hoping she would change her mind and turn around, but in a matter of seconds she had disappeared into the cold.

❄

What could Jený possibly have seen? There was only one way to find out. Ari Thór took the long way back to the hotel, walking via Aðalgata. He stopped outside the building where Unnur's body had been found. Every trace of her fateful fall had now disappeared from the ground. But there still seemed to be an eerie, heavy atmosphere about the place. Perhaps it was the grief of those mourning her death that he could sense hanging in the air. There was almost something menacing about it, though.

Ari Thór looked up to the balcony on the roof. Had she been standing there alone, intending to jump to her death, or had someone been standing behind her and…?

He wasn't going to find any clues in the street. Had he missed something when he had gone out onto the balcony? Something that had also eluded the forensic technicians? He must have walked past this building hundreds of times before without ever really noticing it. What was he not seeing? Could Jenný have noticed something important? She clearly thought so.

Ari Thór was almost certain that there was more to this teenage girl's death than met the eye. Some sort of dark secret lurking out of sight.

Almost without thinking about it, he reached for his phone and called Tómas. They had always worked well together and played off each other's strengths. Tómas had taught Ari Thór that discussing a case and working through the facts and possibilities in their minds was usually the best way to get to the bottom of it. But Ari Thór didn't feel that he could talk about things with Ögmundur in the same way. Perhaps that was why he had been reluctant to involve him more in this investigation.

Ari Thór suspected that his junior officer wasn't planning to stay here forever, that he wanted to earn some experience, but would only do the bare minimum to get it. Maybe Ögmundur was biding his time here in the north until a position opened up in Reykjavík. Ari Thór had to admit he had no idea what the rookie's career plans were; they never talked about that sort of thing.

Tómas picked up the phone on the first ring. 'Ah, Ari Thór,

my boy! What a pleasant surprise.' His friendly voice sounded reassuringly familiar. 'I have to say, I'm a bit tied up at the moment. Is this urgent?'

'Oh, no, don't worry,' Ari Thór replied, feeling sheepish. 'I … I'll call you back later.'

'Well, I've got a couple of minutes, actually. You caught me just before a meeting. I'm still working like a horse, even at my age. Who'd have thought it, eh? Anyway, what's going on? We'll have to get together for a coffee one of these days. I'm long overdue a trip back up north, I know. It's been far too long. So, have the new owners bulldozed my old house and built a new one on top of it?'

'No, it's still standing. But they've done a lot of work on the place. They don't seem to be short on cash.'

'Ah, well, some people have very deep pockets,' Tómas sighed.

'Listen, this is probably too complicated to run by you in a minute or two…'

Ari Thór was hesitant to say anything. He didn't really know why he had called his predecessor. He supposed he had just felt a bit overwhelmed and thought that Tómas might be able to help him see more clearly. It was an old habit, he realised. The time when they had worked together to solve cases had passed. Ari Thór had to stand on his own two feet now.

'Try me,' Tómas said.

'I imagine you've heard about the teenage girl who fell to her death from a balcony in Siglufjörður?' he ventured, all the same.

'Yes,' Tómas replied. 'What a tragedy. I know the family quite well.'

'I'm standing in the street where it happened,' Ari Thór

continued. 'One of the girl's friends walked past here and says she saw something ... something that made her afraid, I think. Something that made her come down to the station and talk to me, in any case. But for the life of me I can't see what it might be.'

'She didn't tell you what it was?' Tómas asked.

'No. She rushed out of the station. She must have been in shock.'

'Send me a photo.'

'A photo?'

'A photo of the place where you are. I'll have a look.'

It would have been hard for Tómas to do much else, Ari Thór realised. He was at the other end of the country and knew nothing about the case. But Ari Thór appreciated the offer. Tómas had always been happy to roll up his sleeves and lend a hand.

'Let's have that coffee together soon, all right?' Tómas insisted.

With a bit of luck, there might be an ulterior motive behind that invitation, Ari Thór hoped. For months he had been wondering whether anything might come of Tómas's offer to put in a word for him for a job in Reykjavík. He wasn't holding out much hope for that anymore, though.

'Yes, let's make it soon,' he agreed. 'And if you can't get up here for some reason, I'll try to come down your way sometime.'

22

Stefnir was still awake, lying beside him. Ari Thór held his son's little hand and smiled every time he opened his eyes, gently reminding him it was time to go to sleep. They had read a short bedtime story together from one of the old children's books the former owners had left in the house. The pages probably hadn't been turned in years. Ari Thór had walked past the bookshelf almost every day since he had moved in, long before Stefnir was born, and he had always seen the collection of classic titles as a treasure to share with his own children one day. His life with Kristín had taken an unexpected turn, but the books hadn't gone anywhere, and it was nice to start putting them to use.

It had been a long, tiring day, but Ari Thór had insisted on being the one to put Stefnir to bed. He had put his heart into reading the bedtime story and thought he might have enjoyed it even more than his son. There was something special – symbolic, even – about this shared moment. In his mind, it seemed to represent all the memories he would never have, all the days of his son's childhood he would miss. There was so much meaning hinging on such a short, little story time. In everyday life, as a normal family, how many hundreds of moments like this would he have taken for granted as day turned into night?

As Stefnir finally dozed off, Ari Thór found himself closing his eyes too, even though he knew he should be getting back to the hotel. He thought about his own father. He'd been doing that a lot lately. Ari Thór could vaguely remember lying next to him in his parents' bed in their old house in

Reykjavík, when he was five or six years old. There was a picture of a similar moment somewhere in one of his family photo albums, so Ari Thór was sure this wasn't a reconstructed memory. It was a snapshot in time, which had continued to pass, as it always did. His father had vanished from his life far too soon. At least he had enjoyed those early childhood years in the family cocoon. And now, while the opportunities might be few and far between, he could help to craft precious memories like those for his own young son.

Time wasn't simply passing anymore; it was flying by. And Ari Thór was living alone in Siglufjörður. Perhaps he could remedy that situation by moving to Sweden, abandoning his career ambitions here for a while and doing something else instead, at least until Kristín had finished her master's and they could return to Iceland. That wasn't a realistic option, though, and he knew it.

He squeezed his son's hand gently, and felt a wave of sleep slowly wash over him too.

❄

Ari Thór woke with a start to find Kristín leaning over him.

'I'm sorry, I didn't mean to frighten you. I just came up to see if everything was all right,' she said softly.

Ari Thór felt groggy, to say the least. He had been in the middle of a curiously realistic dream about his father. In the dream, they had been reunited and were standing face to face. His father had said something to him, but Ari Thór couldn't remember what. All he could recall was a feeling of being filled with happiness.

'No, er, yes … Sorry, I must have drifted off. Give me a second, and I'll be on my way…'

Kristín pressed a gentle hand to his forehead, the way she always used to.

'It's all right, Ari, go back to sleep. I'll sleep downstairs on the sofa tonight.'

There was warmth and even a little affection in her voice, but that was all. Ari Thór knew he shouldn't interpret the gesture as a sign that anything was going to change between them. He appreciated her kindness, though, and smiled at her and nodded. 'Thanks. I'm wiped out.'

She left the room and closed the door behind her.

Ari Thór turned to look at his son sleeping peacefully beside him. Then he carefully took the little boy's hand in his again, and closed his eyes once more.

EASTER SUNDAY

23

It took Ari Thór a second or two to remember why he wasn't in his hotel room when Stefnir woke him early on Easter Sunday morning.

He lifted his son into his arms and carried him downstairs, pausing briefly to unlatch the safety gate he had installed at the top of the staircase to prevent any nasty falls while Stefnir was in the house.

'Here I was, thinking you were going to sleep all day,' Kristín smiled, with a cup of steaming coffee in her hand, as they came into the kitchen. 'Happy Easter.'

'Happy Easter,' Ari Thór replied.

'It's a good thing you slept here last night,' Kristín said. 'You can help Stefnir find his Easter egg.'

She smiled, and Ari Thór remembered fondly what it had been like to be a young boy on Easter morning. His parents always used to hide a chocolate egg for him to find, and he would get up at the crack of dawn to look for it. As soon as he found it, he would start munching on the chocolate and the sweets inside. They even let him drink Coca-Cola at Easter, which was a rare treat indeed back then.

'Fantastic,' he said, turning to Stefnir. 'Are you ready for the special Easter egg hunt? Why don't we start in the living room? That's where all the best hiding places are...'

✳

'Ari Thór, you have to come. *You have to come right now!*'

Salvör's call came just as he was taking his first bite of Easter egg. It had taken them a long time, but they had eventually found Stefnir's egg – in the chandelier hanging in the hallway, curiously. Kristín had very thoughtfully planned ahead and bought Easter eggs for all of them. Maybe it was a way for her to feel like they could still enjoy some semblance of a traditional family life on Easter morning. Maybe she was even warming to the idea of giving things another try, Ari Thór wondered. That said, there was something quite reserved and wooden about her manner. He couldn't quite figure out what it was. But he knew better than to dwell on it. She was probably just anxious for Easter morning to go as smoothly as it could for their little broken family. Yes, it probably wasn't anything more than that. He took the phone into the kitchen, where he could have a more private conversation.

'Calm down, Salvör. Tell me what's happened,' he said.

'Someone … someone broke into my house last night,' she stammered, sounding understandably distraught.

Ari Thór didn't say a word. He had half expected her to pressure him for information about the investigation at some point, and hadn't been looking forward to telling her he still hadn't found any evidence. But he hadn't been expecting her to call and report a break-in.

✳

Ögmundur was already at Salvör's house when Ari Thór got there. Ögmundur was the duty officer that day – and all weekend, for that matter – but in light of the ongoing investigation, circumstances called for Ari Thór to be there too.

Burglaries weren't exactly a common occurrence in the area. *People don't lock their doors at night in Siglufjörður,* Tómas had once told Ari Thór. But apparently that practice was becoming a thing of the past, if Jóhann and Jónína were to be believed. They never used to, but now they did, he remembered them saying the night Unnur's body was found. The cruel beast of modern life was sinking its claws into even the remotest and most isolated of places these days, it seemed.

'I didn't hear a thing,' Salvör said, still trembling in shock, her eyes swollen with tears.

'He smashed a window by the back door,' Ögmundur explained. 'Probably so he could reach in and turn the latch.'

'Has anything been stolen?' Ari Thór asked Salvör.

'I'm not sure, I haven't really looked everywhere. I don't think anything is missing, but … still, that seems strange, doesn't it? There's all sorts of stuff worth taking here. Nothing particularly valuable, mind you, just the kind of thing a burglar would snatch. But it looks like nothing's been touched.'

'Are you sure someone actually came into the house?'

Ögmundur took it upon himself to speak for Salvör. 'I don't think there's any question about that, is there? Unless…'

He didn't finish his sentence, but Ari Thór guessed what he was going to say before he stopped himself: *Unless Salvör staged the break-in herself.*

'Ari Thór, I think he must have gone into her bedroom…' Salvör murmured.

'Unnur's room?'

'Yes, it looks like some things might have been moved

around in there. But I don't know … I don't know why someone would want to do that. And I don't know if he took anything, either…'

'He? Are you sure it was a man?' Ari Thór looked at Salvör first, then turned to Ögmundur, who shook his head.

'I don't know,' Salvör eventually said.

The two police officers went to the back door, where they looked at the broken window, then they made their way upstairs to Unnur's room. Ari Thór took a good look around the room, making sure not to touch anything. He had a strange feeling that someone had been here, as Salvör claimed, but he couldn't tell whether anything had been taken.

'You said you didn't see anything, Salvör? You didn't wake up at all?' Ari Thór asked, once the three of them were sitting at the kitchen table.

She shook her head.

'No, not at all. I don't have a clue what time it happened.'

'Think very carefully. I imagine the burglar might have been looking for Unnur's laptop or phone, but we still have those. Was there anything else in your daughter's room that might be of particular significance, that might … that might explain what happened?' Ari Thór didn't want to say too much.

Salvör put her head in her hands and choked back tears. 'No, not that I can think of. I've said it before and I'll say it again: she was just a normal teenager. She was never any trouble to me at all. She worked hard at school, and getting good grades was all that mattered to her. She was an angel.'

Then she added: 'And she kept nothing from me. She didn't have any secrets.'

This time, Ari Thór didn't believe her for a second.

24

Ögmundur drove back to the police station, and Ari Thór walked. As soon he set foot in the door, his junior officer had a message to relay to him.

'You just missed a call from the elderly couple who live in the building where Unnur's body was found,' Ögmundur said.

'What did they say?'

'They wanted to talk to you. I told them you'd call them back.'

'Seriously? Couldn't you just take care of it?'

Ari Thór didn't bother to hide his frustration. He just wanted to get back home to see Kristín and Stefnir.

'I had nothing to say to them. It was the woman who called. I can't remember what her name was.'

'Jónína.'

'That's it. She wanted to know how the investigation was going. I got the sense she was worried. Maybe a bit too much. Did she know the girl?'

Ari Thór shook his head in despair.

'All right, I'll go and pay them a visit.'

❊

When Jónína opened the door, Ari Thór couldn't help but notice how tired she looked. She ushered him into the living room of the ground-floor flat, and promptly sat down on the sofa beside the window, like she had the last time. The room was just as gloomy as it had been. Jóhann was nowhere to be seen.

Ari Thór sat down in an armchair across from her.

'My husband is out,' Jónína said, as if she could tell what Ari Thór was thinking. 'He always goes to the pool at this time. He didn't like the idea of me calling you.'

'Why not?'

'He says this whole thing has nothing to do with us. We might never have spoken to Unnur herself, but we know her mother a bit. Everyone knows everyone here. I'm sure you've gathered that by now. I still can't get over what happened. It's terrible.'

Ari Thór nodded. The ensuing silence dragged on, and he didn't have all day to sit here.

'You said everyone knows everyone. Have you ever met the two men who live out in Siglunes?'

A look of surprise flashed across Jónína's face.

'Yes, I know Thorleifur well. The father, I mean. We were at school together. He's a man with a heart of gold. Why do you ask?'

'Just out of curiosity. I went up the fjord in a boat yesterday and met him and his son. It's a nice place they have there.'

'Oh, I haven't been for years. And I've never gone there by water. I used to like hiking the trail when I was younger, but I don't have the strength to be bounding over the rocks like a mountain goat these days.'

Now that he had broken the ice, Ari Thór cut to the chase. 'Was there something you wanted to tell me about Unnur, Jónína?'

'Something to tell you? What makes you think that?'

'I was just wondering if you'd called me because you'd forgotten to mention some detail the other night,' Ari Thór explained. 'People often do, when something terrible like this happens. It can be hard for them to think of everything at the time, but then when they get over the initial shock, the details might start to trickle back to them.'

Jónína shook her head. 'No, no, it's nothing like that. I…' She paused. Ari Thór waited.

'I was worried, that's all. It was me who buzzed the door open that night. It was me who let her into the building. I've been losing sleep over it ever since.'

'That's understandable,' he replied.

Ari Thór couldn't see how he could help the elderly woman get through this ordeal. The fact was, she had enabled Unnur to gain access to the balcony from where she had, by all appearances, thrown herself to her death.

'Do you think she would have done it anyway?' Jónína asked. 'I dread to think about … having such a terrible thing on my conscience, you see.'

In a split second, it occurred to Ari Thór that all this might be a performance for his benefit. Were the elderly couple on the ground floor hiding something from him? How plausible was it that this woman might feel she was to blame for the suicide of a teenage girl? Ari Thór couldn't rule out the possibility that she had some other burden of guilt to carry. Over time he had come to expect the worst of people, rather than the best.

What if Unnur had come to pay Jóhann or Jónína a visit that night? And what if the visit had taken a turn for the worse? Or maybe it was something to do with the historian who lived in the flat upstairs. Ari Thór thought he'd better speak to the man again.

'You know, Jónína,' he ended up saying. 'I've been a police officer for a number of years, and I was a student of theology before that. From experience, I can assure you that you are in no way responsible for what happened. You just did what anyone else could have done. People in a small town like ours don't tend to suspect their neighbours – or even perfect strangers. You couldn't have known who was ringing the doorbell, and there's no way you could have imagined what was going through that poor young woman's mind. Unfortunately, we'll probably never know. I think you can sleep easy.'

Ari Thór surprised himself. He hadn't been intending to deliver a speech. He didn't actually believe most of what he'd said, but his words clearly made Jónína feel better. And that in itself he found heartwarming.

Jónína gave him a shy smile. 'I'm so sorry, I haven't offered you anything to eat or drink. My mind's all over the place. I can make you a coffee if you like, and I must have some biscuits somewhere in the kitchen.'

'Oh, please don't put yourself out. I'll have to be on my way soon, anyway. You wouldn't happen to know if Bjarki is back from Reykjavík yet, would you?'

'Yes, he came back last night,' Jónína replied.

'I think I'll pay him a quick visit while I'm here. Do you know if he's home at the moment?'

'I heard some noise upstairs earlier, so I imagine he might be.'

'Very well. Thank you for your time. And please give me a call if anything comes back to you. You never know.'

'Yes … yes, I will, she nodded.

'And do give Jóhann my regards.'

Ari Thór saw himself out.

25

The impromptu visit seemed to catch Bjarki by surprise, but he invited Ari Thór to come in without a second's hesitation.

'Sorry about the mess, I was working. Come through to the living room.'

He moved a pile of books off the sofa to make room for Ari Thór to sit down.

Bjarki was quite a tall man with a thick head of hair and small, round glasses perched on the end of his nose. He looked to be somewhere around forty. His broad shoulders and tanned complexion clashed with the image one might have of a man who must spend days on end immersed in books. He had charisma, that much was clear, and would make a good professor or politician, Ari Thór thought, as he sat down on the sofa. Furnished with antiques, the flat felt cosy and welcoming.

Bjarki didn't offer him anything to drink. *The man has no manners*, Ari Thór thought to himself. The unannounced visit didn't seem to bother him, however, even though he surely had better things to do than talk to the police. Ari Thór wasn't planning to stay long, in any case. He had just thought he would kill two birds with one stone, as he had been downstairs with Jónína already.

'Nice place,' Ari Thór said, to break the ice. 'Do you own the flat?' He recalled that Jóhann and Jónína had told him the house used to belong to Bjarki's grandparents before it was converted into flats.

'In a way, yes,' Bjarki replied. 'It's in my father's name. I was born here, actually, but until recently I'd never lived here as an adult. Still, I have to say, I feel very much at home here. As I think I've told you, I've been awarded some funding by the town council to write about residents of Siglufjörður who emigrated to North America at the end of the nineteenth century – but that's not my only field of expertise, of course.'

'Are you working full time on that project?' Ari Thór was doubtful.

'More or less.'

'Why that topic in particular?' Ari Thór continued.

Bjarki's face lit up. 'Because I'm a historian, and that was a fascinating time in Iceland's history. Not many people have taken an interest in it locally. Did you know that people from around here had been a part of that wave of emigration?'

'To be honest, until a few days ago, I had no idea.'

Ari Thór was not exactly a history buff. He preferred to spend what little spare time he had listening to music and trying to clear his mind so that he could live in the moment, rather than dwell on the past.

'I've been passionate about the period since I was in high school, if not before. We don't know exactly how many Icelanders went over there, but there were at least fourteen thousand. If not more.'

'And the Siglufjörður town council is funding the project, you say?'

'Yes. It's not the first time they've given me a grant, actually. They paid me handsomely to write about the heyday of herring fishing a few years ago,' he added, his chest swelling with pride.

'Oh, really?'

'Well, my father is from Siglufjörður. Like I said, I was born here, in the north, and we lived here before we moved to Reykjavík. My family used to work in the herring.

Everyone did back in those days. The fishery collapsed before I was born, but my dad used to tell me all kinds of stories. Enough to fill a book. Living up here, you must have heard all about the golden age of the herring fishery, I imagine?'

Ari Thór nodded. 'Yes, people talk about it all the time. Especially how it disappeared.'

'It happened pretty much overnight. People who had invested money in the industry ended up with empty pockets. The banks seized the property of anyone who couldn't pay their debts, and life basically ground to a standstill. I'm not very active politically, but my old man, who's quite conservative in his politics, told me it killed the enterprising spirit in the town. He never wanted to live here again after what happened. I think he lost a lot when the fishery collapsed. And we went to live in the capital when I was a small boy.'

'And now you're back,' Ari Thór said.

'Yes, I...' He paused, almost subconsciously. 'This place gives me a good feeling. The flat is nice and comfortable, and I've got plenty of good memories here. There's more life in the town than there ever used to be, too. What with the tourists, the investors bringing money in from outside the community, and the cultural scene that's really taking off...'

'Yes, the place does have its charm,' Ari Thór said, getting up from the sofa.

He was enjoying talking to Bjarki. He could have seen them becoming friends, in different circumstances. Ari Thór wasn't especially close to anyone in Siglufjörður – not around his age, at least. He had spent most of his time with Tómas, before he moved away, and the Reverend Eggert, but they were both of a different generation. That hadn't been an issue while Kristín was still around; they'd always had each other for company despite the storms that blew through the house most days. But things were different now.

'It's ideal for writing,' Bjarki added.

'Are you planning to stay here for a while?' Ari Thór asked.

'Well, the funding won't run out until next year at the earliest. I'm planning to head to Canada in the autumn, to follow in the footsteps of the Icelanders who went over there. I'll stay there and write for a few weeks. But other than that, I'll be here. I don't want to miss the nicest time of the year in Siglufjörður.'

'Oh, good. Maybe we could get together for a coffee sometime, then,' Ari Thór suggested. 'I wouldn't mind hearing a bit more about the locals who crossed an ocean to start a new life in North America. When all this is cleared up, of course.'

Bjarki smiled. 'With pleasure.'

Maybe it was something in the man's tone of voice, or maybe his smile didn't quite ring true, but Ari Thór suddenly felt uneasy. *Never trust anyone,* he thought. It was time to dig a little deeper.

'You said on the phone that you were at a conference, didn't you?'

'That's right,' Bjarki replied.

'What was it about?'

'Research methodology and data sources. It was organised by the university. Not exactly riveting stuff, unless you're a research nerd.'

Guessing what Ari Thór must be wanting to know, he added: 'I gave a presentation during the day on Wednesday, and I was part of a panel discussion that evening. As usual, there was a dinner afterwards, and everyone went to the pub for a drink after that.'

Ari Thór knew what he was really saying: *I was in Reykjavík all day on Wednesday, and I was out late drinking that night in the city – not in my flat, right above where that girl was found dead in the street.*

'What about your time off?' Ari Thór asked.

'My time off?' Bjarki seemed confused.

'You told me you were going to enjoy a few days off in Reykjavík after the conference.'

'Right. Yes, of course. I have to admit, I had a change of heart. After you called, I decided I'd rather come home instead. I felt a bit on edge about what you said had happened, so I wanted to make sure everything was all right here at the flat, you see…'

'And did you notice anything unusual when you got home?'

'No.' Bjarki shook his head. 'Turns out I was worried for nothing.'

'Well, be sure to let me know if something does occur to you later.'

'Of course,' he replied smoothly. Then, with none of his earlier self-assurance, he added: 'You don't think … someone pushed her, do you?'

Ari Thór considered his words carefully. 'At the moment, there's nothing to suggest that.'

'But you're still conducting an investigation?'

'An investigation? Of course,' Ari Thór replied. 'I want to know exactly what happened. For her mother's sake, if nothing else.'

'That's understandable,' Bjarki nodded.

'Well, thank you for your time,' Ari Thór concluded.

'You're welcome. I'll look forward to that coffee.'

26

'The weather's taking a turn for the worse.'

That was the first thing Kristín said to Ari Thór as he walked in the door. He had been thrilled to get back to see them, but she was obviously in a darker mood.

'I think we should head back today,' she added.

'Today?'

Ari Thór's heart sank. Now he regretted not handing the investigation over to Ögmundur. What an idiot he had been to waste time on a case that wasn't going anywhere while he could have been enjoying every moment with his son. Kristín said the winter storm was blowing in more quickly than forecast and was now expected to hit the region as early as the next morning. Now that he thought about it, Ari Thór had noticed quite a bit of traffic driving out of town – more than he would have expected before the end of the long weekend. Siglufjörður was a charming place to visit, but it still had a reputation for vicious blizzards and the tourists didn't want to risk getting snowed in.

'I've already changed our flights. We're leaving Akureyri for Reykjavík tonight.'

'What? When are you packing up and leaving here, then?' Ari Thór tried to hide the disappointment in his voice. He already knew what the answer would be.

'Right now, Ari. I was waiting for you to get home so we could say goodbye. I've packed our bags. They're already in the car.'

'But…'

He wanted to say so many things, but the words were stuck in his throat.

'You've only just got here,' he managed to say. 'We've barely spent any time together.'

'That's the way it is,' Kristín replied. 'There are some things we can't control, you know.'

Ari Thór was grateful at least that she didn't bemoan his repeated absences for work that weekend.

'We'll catch up properly another time,' she said, pulling him into a hug. 'You will come and see us this summer, won't you? It's not that long to wait.'

She sounded like she was talking to a child, Ari Thór thought. That seemed quite fitting, given how small he felt right now.

'Yes, of course. I've already booked my flight.'

'The weather's warmer in Sweden in July than it is here, you know.'

'Don't knock summer in Siglufjörður,' he said, intending the words to come out more light-heartedly than they did.

Then he knelt beside his son, pulled him close and hugged him tight.

27

Ari Thór had asked Ögmundur to investigate the break-in, but he wasn't holding out much hope. As far as they could see, the perpetrator had left no trace, and no witnesses had come forward. The more time that went by, the less likely they were to find out who had broken into Salvör's home.

Meanwhile, there was one more person Ari Thór had to talk to in connection with Unnur's death: her friend Sara. As soon as Kristín and Stefnir had driven away, he had given her a call, figuring that work would help to take his mind off things.

Sara had suggested they meet at the café she was working in over the Easter holidays. It was a popular place, renowned for its hot chocolate, and it was especially busy now. Ari Thór arrived to find people queueing out of the door. When he walked in, a young woman waved and beckoned him over.

'Hello, you must be Ari Thór,' she said. 'I'm Sara. I've arranged to go on my break now; we can talk in the back.'

She smiled with her eyes and offered him a hot chocolate, on the house. Ari Thór was only too happy to accept.

'I apologise for bothering you while you're at work,' he said.

'Don't worry; it'll do me good to catch my breath for a few minutes. It's crazy busy here. But I can't complain. At least I'm earning a bit of money over the school holidays.'

'Is this your last year in high school?' Ari Thór asked.

'Yes.'

'What are you planning to do next year?'

'I'll be moving away. I'm going to university in Reykjavík to study engineering.'

'And after that, do you think you'll come back to Siglufjörður?'

She gave him a knowing look, as if to say, *what do you think?*

'I understand you and Unnur knew each other well,' Ari Thór said, taking a sip of his chocolate.

'Yes, quite well,' Sara replied.

'Would you say she was your best friend?'

'I wouldn't go that far. She didn't have a lot of friends. We were just classmates, really. I suppose we just fell into working together on school assignments. We didn't really see each other out of school though.'

'Did she have a boyfriend? Or a girlfriend?'

'Neither. I don't think so, anyway. I'd be surprised if she did. She always kept herself to herself. She was a nice girl. Serious and hardworking, but friendly and approachable. She was a good person, if you ask me.'

'Was she ever depressed?'

Sara thought for a moment. 'I don't know. I don't think I'm the right person to ask. She didn't really show her emotions. But now that you mention it, maybe she had been a bit more distant than usual, these last few weeks. Distracted, somehow.'

'How do you mean?'

'It was as if she had her head in the clouds. I've always thought of her as someone who had her feet firmly on the ground, but something subtle shifted in her. I can't quite put my finger on it, though.'

'Your name crops up a lot in her diary. Mostly in relation to homework,' Ari Thór said, reluctant to elaborate for fear of saying too much. 'But I was given the impression you two knew each other better than that…'

The smile on Sara's lips froze and turned to an expression of surprise. 'I ... Yes, maybe that was how she saw things. I don't know ... she probably didn't have any other friends at school. I hate to say it, but...'

'And what do *your* friends think about all this? Do you have any ideas about what happened? Any theories?'

Sara shrugged. 'What is there to say? Of course, it's tragic, but we have no idea what happened. It just ... happened, that's all. Obviously, her death has shocked us all, but as far as I know, no one knows or suspects any more than you do ... Unless...'

She fell silent.

'Sara,' Ari Thór said softly, choosing his words carefully. 'It's entirely possible that Unnur killed herself, and we may never know the reasons why. However, if there is the slightest hint of anything criminal about her death, it is absolutely crucial that we pursue every lead. Do you see what I'm saying?'

She cast a furtive glance around to make sure no one else was listening. They were sitting in the small staff kitchen at the back of the café. Even here Ari Thór could smell the heady aroma of chocolate in the air and hear the clattering of dishes and cutlery on the other side of the wall. The place was buzzing with life. Obviously not all the tourists in town had decided to hasten their departure ahead of the storm.

'Well, I was wondering...' Sara began. 'There's this girl in our class, Jenný ... Do you know her?'

'I know who you're talking about,' Ari Thór replied, as neutrally as possible. He wasn't about to let slip that Jenný had come to see him at the police station.

'She took it very personally, from what I've heard,' Sara continued. 'I thought that was strange, because she and

Unnur didn't really talk to one another. I'm not sure, but …
maybe she knows something. Don't tell her I was the one who
told you, though. I don't want to get mixed up in all this.'

'Of course not,' Ari Thór assured her.

'I have to get back to work now. It's busy out there.' She
stood. This conversation was over.

'I understand. Thanks for taking the time to answer my
questions, Sara. You've been very helpful.'

Ari Thór saw himself out of the crowded café. He took a
deep breath as he stepped out into the bitterly cold air.

28

After he left the café, Ari Thór decided to go out of his way and pay a visit to Gudjón Helgason, the artist who had reported finding Unnur's body, at his lodgings on the edge of town. Ögmundur had taken the man's statement at the station the morning after the death, but nothing major had come to light. Ari Thór was sure, though, that there was more to the artist's nocturnal wanderings than met the eye. And there was no time like the present for clearing up lingering doubts.

The address Gudjón had given led him to a small wooden house on the shore, one of many old, shack-like buildings that had been meticulously renovated as holiday homes in recent years.

Ari Thór knocked at the door and waited for longer than he would have expected before Gudjón opened up, dressed only in lounge shorts and a loose singlet.

'Oh, hello there,' he yawned. 'The inspector calls, I see. I wasn't expecting you.'

'I was passing by,' Ari Thór explained. 'Can I come in?'

'Be my guest.'

Gudjón stepped aside and Ari Thór wiped his boots on his way in.

'It's a nice little place, isn't it?' Gudjón continued. 'Have you been here before? Perhaps while another artist was staying here?'

'No, but I've walked past this house more times than I can count,' Ari Thór replied.

Gudjón led the way into a small, tidy living room that was

furnished tastefully with antiques. The spectacular view of the fjord from the window only added to the charm of the place.

'The studio is downstairs, in the basement. There's a whole workshop down there. It's not a bad thing actually. Obviously, the light is better in this room, but I think the view would be too distracting for me to paint and create up here. Not too shabby a place, is it? The owners are a pair of lawyers who live in Reykjavík. They come up here in the summer and let artists use the place in the winter. I must admit, I don't usually have much patience for lawyers, but I'm grateful to them for this at least. They've bought an old abandoned lighthouse on the other side of the fjord too, apparently. They're fixing it up so they can have artists' retreats over there as well.'

'I hadn't heard,' Ari Thór replied. 'Is that on the point, by Siglunes?'

'No, it's only about halfway up the shore on the way to Siglunes. The lighthouse was decommissioned years ago.'

Ari Thór wasn't planning to stay long, so he remained standing.

'I'm afraid I don't have much to tell you other than that,' Gudjón continued. 'I've already told you and your colleague everything I know.'

'Let's go over that again, shall we?' Ari Thór resisted the urge to correct the man: *My junior officer, not my colleague.*

'I came up here for a three-month stay.' Gudjón sighed wearily. 'My time's nearly up, so I'll have to give back the keys soon. Don't worry, you'll be rid of me in a few days' time.'

Ari Thór ignored the man's attempt at small talk. 'You've probably heard that the young woman who died was called Unnur.'

'I saw her name in the paper, yes.'

'Do you know her?' Ari Thór pressed.

'No, I told you that already. I hardly know anyone in this town. I've crossed paths with a few local artists, and have a drink with them sometimes, but they're little more than acquaintances, really. And even then, I can count them all on the fingers of one hand.'

'Unnur's mother is named Salvör,' Ari Thór continued. 'Have you met her?'

Gudjón frowned and shook his head vigorously. 'No. Do the local police make a habit of trying to drag visitors into disrepute when something like this happens? Didn't she simply throw herself off a balcony? I don't see anything suspicious about that…'

'What I want to know, Gudjón, is what you were doing right there in the middle of the night.'

'I didn't know I was living in a police state. I was out for a stroll, that's all. I find my creative juices flow more freely at night.'

With an air of indignation, he added: 'I wouldn't expect you to understand.'

Ari Thór chose to ignore the comment. 'Did you see anything that caught your eye? Did you happen to notice anyone else in proximity to the scene, for instance?'

'In proximity to the scene? Oh, for God's sake, why all the formalities! You really should try and loosen up a little, man.'

Ari Thór bit his tongue and took a deep breath. There was no point insisting. This interview was going nowhere. Gudjón might well be telling the truth, he thought. But one thing was for sure: Ari Thór had no desire to see or speak to this man ever again.

29

Ari Thór was sitting at the piano in his living room on Eyrargata when Tómas called. The wind was blowing hard outside already, and if the weather forecast was to be believed, the dark, snow-laden storm clouds would not be far behind.

Ari Thór answered the phone, allowing himself to cross his fingers for a second, in the hope his predecessor was calling to offer him a job in the city. He hadn't brought it up when they spoke the previous day, but he did wonder if Tómas's insistence that they catch up soon was a sign that something might be in the works. In all honesty, Ari Thór wasn't sure how he would respond if such an opportunity were to come his way, but there was something exciting about entertaining the possibility.

'Hello?'

'Hello, Ari Thór. It's Tómas. Am I bothering you? Oh, and Happy Easter, by the way.'

'Not at all. Same to you too.'

'Sorry, I was up to my eyes in work yesterday when you called. But I gave your case some thought when I got up this morning.'

'So, what do you think?'

'Well, I had a look at the photo you texted me. Nothing really jumped out at me, other than the fact that seeing Siglufjörður in the background made me feel homesick and want to drive right back there.' He chuckled. 'The young lady who came to see you, she told you she saw something, did she?'

'That's right.'

'Is that the way she put it? Were those the exact words she used?'

'Yes, well … what are you getting at?'

'Maybe it was *someone* she saw, not something.'

Ari Thór had to think about it. Tómas might well be right, but he couldn't recall exactly what Jenný had said.

'Maybe…' he replied, remembering now that she hadn't actually finished her sentence.

'It's funny, but I miss being so far away from you, Ari Thór,' Tómas said. 'I wish we could investigate cases together like we did before. We made a pretty good team, didn't we?'

'A very good team, I'd say.' Ari Thór found himself smiling.

'How are things going with the young rookie? What's his name again?'

'Ögmundur.'

'Ögmundur, yes. I don't know him. Do you know who his people are?' Tómas asked. The custom was slowly dying out, but many Icelanders were still in the habit of asking strangers which family lines they descended from.

'Not really. All I know is that none of his ancestors were police officers. He told me that once.'

'So he's the first cop in the family. Like you.'

'Like me, yes.'

'And how is it going, working with him?'

Ari Thór paused for thought.

'Perfectly well,' he lied, though he was sure he hadn't fully managed to hide what he really thought.

'Glad to hear it. It warms my heart to see how well you've adapted to life in the north. You've really made the place your home. It's reassuring for me to know that someone so competent has stepped into my shoes.'

'How are things down there with you?' Ari Thór hastened to ask. 'Are they keeping you busy?'

'Oh, they certainly are, my boy. Unfortunately for me. I wish things were as quiet in Reykjavík as they are in Siglufjörður. At my age, I should be able to sit back and relax a bit, don't you think?' he laughed. 'Anyway, I'd best not keep my wife waiting. We're going out for brunch, as people down here say. A rather late brunch, actually, now that I see the time. In Siglufjörður, we used to eat breakfast in the morning, and lunch around noon. And that was always at home. We never went out. But maybe that's starting to change there too, like so many other things…'

'I imagine so,' Ari Thór replied pensively. 'Things change. They always do.'

'I'll talk to you soon, my boy.' And with that, Tómas hung up.

Ari Thór stood for a moment, holding the phone in his hand, staring into the distance. Tómas had given him food for thought, but he hadn't said a word about any future job prospects in the capital. Ari Thór suspected he had waited too long to ask. The way Tómas was talking, he obviously saw him as his long-term successor. It was as if he had ruled out the possibility that his former protégé might want to move on from Siglufjörður one day.

That was it, then, Ari Thór thought.

He was stuck here, whether he liked it or not.

30

'Hello, this is Hersir,' the doctor announced in a less than amenable way at the other end of the line.

'Good evening, Hersir, this is Inspector Ari Thór Arason.'

It was dinner time, and Ari Thór was at a loss as to what to do with himself. His plans for the rest of the weekend had gone up in smoke when Kristín and Stefnir had decided to leave earlier than planned. He had a leg of lamb in the fridge and had been planning to roast it for them if they had decided to stay in that night rather than dine out, but he had no desire to get into preparing a joint of meat and all the trimmings just for himself. Instead, he had settled for a slice of toast and decided to pick up the phone.

'Yes, of course, Ari Thór,' Hersir replied, with no more warmth in his voice.

'I was wondering if you had any news about Hávardur. You said you were going to ask his son if he wouldn't mind me talking to his father.'

'Oh, really? Did I?'

Ari Thór couldn't believe what he was hearing. Had the doctor really forgotten his promise, or was he trying to weasel his way out of the question?

'About what he wrote on the wall of his room…?'

'Ah, yes, of course,' Hersir replied. 'I do apologise. I thought all that was behind us. I was under the impression you yourself had given us the go-ahead to clean the wall.'

'Nevertheless, I'd still like to speak with him. Have you contacted his son?'

'No. I didn't want to bother him, with it being Easter…'

'No problem. I'll take care of it,' Ari Thór replied.

'Well, perhaps it would be better if…'

'I imagine you'll have his name, phone number and address?' Ari Thór wasn't taking no for an answer.

'His name is Thormódur,' Hersir replied, with some reluctance. 'Thormódur Hávardarson. He lives on the same street as you.'

'Perfect, that will be enough for me to track him down.'

'Listen, don't…'

'Yes?'

'Don't make it any worse for him than you have to. His father is in an advanced state of dementia, and that's hard enough for him to deal with, so it would be best not to…'

'Twist the knife in the wound?'

'Yes, exactly.'

'Thank you for your assistance, Hersir. I'll come and see you again if I have to.'

'You're w—'

But Ari Thór had already hung up.

31

Ari Thór decided to go and knock at Thormódur Hávardarson's door unannounced rather than pick up the phone. He was greeted by a tall, slim man who, other than being almost completely bald, didn't look a day over fifty. Ari Thór explained to the man, as briefly as he could, that his father might know someone connected to the young woman who was found dead a few nights earlier. Thormódur saw no reason why Ari Thór shouldn't talk to the elderly man.

'It's not easy to have a conversation with him, though,' was all he cautioned. 'He tends to confuse things that just happened and things that happened years ago. It's all mixed up in his mind.'

'Does he imagine things?' Ari Thór asked.

'What do you mean?'

'Does he talk nonsense, or do the things he says seem to be grounded in reality? To a certain extent, obviously.'

Thormódur reflected for a moment before he answered.

'I go to see him every day. I'm lucky to have him close to me, here in Siglufjörður. The authorities wanted to send him away to a home in Akureyri, until Hersir stepped in and saved the day. I'm infinitely grateful to the man. To my knowledge, Dad has never spoken a word of nonsense. There's truth in everything he says. You just never know if what he's talking about happened yesterday or sixty years ago.'

❄

By nightfall, the storm was closing in fast. Dark, ominous clouds rolled across the sky, obscuring the stars, leaving no doubt as to what was coming. Still, Ari Thór decided to brave the imminent blizzard and walk up the hill to the care home to try and have a word with Hávardur.

Hersir was nowhere to be seen. Fortunately, Ugla was there to greet him.

'Oh, hi there!' she exclaimed. It was obvious from the look in her eye that this was a pleasant surprise. 'It's nice to see so much of you these days.'

Ari Thór smiled, but he didn't really know what to say. He wasn't sure how formal he should be, given that he was here for work.

'Is Hávardur here?' he asked, a bit too mechanically.

'Yes, he's still with us. He's not going anywhere.' Ugla smiled. 'You're lucky, he's still awake.'

'Oh, I know he's not really going anywhere,' Ari Thór replied, somewhat awkwardly. 'I just thought maybe his son might pick him up sometimes and take him out for a walk or a visit somewhere, that's all.'

'His son? No, he comes to visit all the time, but they never go out anywhere.'

'Anyway, how is Hávardur doing today?'

'So far, so good.'

'He … he hasn't started writing on his wall again, then?'

'No, and he hasn't said a word about it either. It's as if he's completely forgotten what happened.'

Hávardur was sitting in a wheelchair in the lounge, watching a programme on the public TV channel. Well, his eyes were turned towards the screen, but Ari Thór couldn't tell if the elderly man was paying any attention to it.

'Hávardur,' Ugla said softly. 'This is Ari Thór. He's with the police. He'd like to have a little chat with you.'

The elderly man's eyes sparked to life. He turned first to Ugla, then to Ari Thór. He seemed to be in remarkably good health for his age, with an expressive face and what looked to be strong muscles on his bones. There wasn't a single hair on his head. Clearly, his heavily balding son was headed the same way.

'Ari Thór?' he said in a weak, hoarse voice.

'Yes, my name is Ari Thór.'

'Who are your people, son?'

'I'm from Reykjavík,' Ari Thór replied.

'Yes, but who are your parents?' Hávardur insisted.

Ari Thór glanced at Ugla. She smiled, as if to say he would have to answer Hávardur's questions before he got to ask any questions of his own.

'My father's name was Ari Thór Arason too. He was an accountant. And my mother Hafdís was a musician. She used to play with the Icelandic Symphony Orchestra.'

Hávardur remained silent for a moment, as if giving the information time to sink in.

'I listen to the symphony orchestra a lot on the radio. I even went to see them once, in Reykjavík. It was … why yes, it was just last year.'

'And did you enjoy it?'

Hávardur gave Ari Thór a blank look. 'Enjoy what?'

'Seeing the symphony orchestra.'

Hávardur shook his head. 'Oh yes, I enjoyed it very much.'

Ari Thór couldn't help but smile. With a bit of luck, the elderly man might be coming back to his senses. 'Why don't you tell me all about it,' he said.

'With pleasure,' Hávardur replied, adopting a teacherly air. 'I remember the church bells rang out.'

'The church bells?'

'Yes, it was very strange. Very unusual, as you can imagine … in the middle of the night, I tell you.'

'The bells rang out in the middle of the night? When?'

'Well, during the earthquake, of course. It all but shook our house to pieces. I thought I'd end up buried in the rubble. We all ran out into the street. Me, my parents and my brothers and sisters. We didn't dare go back inside afterwards. And then obviously, the power went out.'

Ari Thór looked up at Ugla, who leaned closer to whisper in his ear. 'He often tells that story.'

Then she turned to Hávardur. 'Wasn't that in 1963? The great earthquake?'

'Exactly!' the elderly man roared. He gave Ari Thór a mischievous wink. 'She knows all about that.'

Ari Thór cleared his throat. His doubts that this conversation would lead anywhere were growing. 'Actually, I'd like to ask you a few questions about something else, Hávardur.'

'Go on, then.'

'The other night, you wrote something on the wall of your room. Do you remember that?'

'On the wall?' Hávardur's face darkened into a storm cloud.

Ari Thór turned to Ugla, who shrugged.

'"She was murdered", Hávardur, that's what you wrote,' he continued.

'What I wrote? Me? Who's been murdered?'

'That's precisely what I was hoping you could tell me.'

Hávardur froze for a second, then hung his head.

'It was a teenage girl who died,' Ari Thór explained, watching for a reaction.

Suddenly, the elderly man sat bolt upright in his wheelchair. 'No, no. It wasn't her. I saw what happened, and it wasn't her.'

A shiver ran through Ari Thór.

Hávardur looked and sounded so sure of his affirmation. There was no haunting wistfulness to these words. He had witnessed something that was still fresh in his mind. The only thing was, from his room at the care home, he could not have seen the street where Unnur's body was found. Clearly, he had not been an eyewitness to the teenage girl's death.

Now the elderly man's eyes glazed over with a faraway look. Staring into space, he seemed completely oblivious to Ari Thór's presence.

'Who was it, then?' Ari Thór asked.

No answer.

'Who was it, Hávardur?' he insisted. It came out more harshly than he had intended. 'Who did you see?'

Still no reaction. Ari Thór tried a different tack.

'Hávardur?' he called, to draw his attention. 'Who killed her?'

The old man's eyes flickered to life, suggesting he had understood the question. Ari Thór had established a connection.

'Who? … Finnbogi. It was *Finnbogi!*' Hávardur cried, with a flash of agitation.

'What did he do?' Ari Thór coaxed. 'What did Finnbogi do?'

'He *murdered* her,' the elderly man barked, in no uncertain terms.

Then he lowered his head and looked quizzically at Ari Thór. 'Who are you, young man?'

'It's Ari Thór,' Ugla reminded him kindly. 'He just came to say hello and have a quick word with you.'

'I'm sorry, pal. I don't remember you. Do we know each other?'

Ari Thór shook his head. 'No, not really. I'm sorry to have troubled you. I'll leave you in peace.'

They left Hávardur sitting in front of the television and went to sit in the staff kitchen.

'I'd forgotten your mother played in the symphony orchestra,' Ugla said. 'Fancy a coffee?'

'I'd love one, thanks.'

'You did tell me at the time, I remember that. When we were playing piano together.'

'When you were teaching me, you mean. Perhaps not with the greatest of success,' Ari Thór teased.

'Ah, so that's why your lessons ended so abruptly, then, is it?' she chuckled.

It was reassuring for Ari Thór to hear Ugla joking about the course their relationship had taken – if that's what they could call it. She certainly hadn't always made light of the situation. For a long time she had looked away whenever they crossed paths in the street.

'Are you still practising?' she asked.

'Only a little now and then. I haven't taken any more lessons, but I do my best to read the notes and play a few simple pieces. It doesn't sound too bad, at least to my ears.'

'You were always pretty good, as I remember. You've got an ear for music, you know,' she said with a smile.

'I get that from my mother.' Ari Thór barely whispered the words. It made him feel vulnerable to talk about something he usually kept to himself.

'She was a violinist, wasn't she?'

'That's right.'

'I remember now. Did she often play for you?'

Ari Thór nodded. 'Sometimes, she used to do recitals – little private performances – just for my father and me. I'll never forget them – they were … precious experiences. And she would always have her violin out to practise, of course, but that wasn't the same thing. Sometimes, she would take me along to see the orchestra play. Not very often, though. Not often enough. Maybe she was planning to introduce me to all that when I was a bit older…'

Ugla was about to reply when Hávardur called out from the TV room. She got up.

'He's calling for me, but he can never remember my name. I have to see what he wants. I'm sorry, Ari Thór, but can we continue this conversation later on?'

'Yes, of course.'

She pulled him into a hug and kissed him on the cheek.

'Unfortunately, I'll be on duty for the rest of the Easter weekend,' she said. 'But I'm free tomorrow night…' she added, after a short pause.

Now it was Ari Thór's turn to hesitate. He thought about Kristín. The woman he thought he was going to spend the rest of his life with. But nothing lasted forever, he realised. Maybe the time had come to move on. He couldn't spend his life waiting and hoping.

'Tomorrow night?' he replied, pretending to check his mental calendar. 'I think I can manage that.'

She smiled. 'Perfect. How about my place, eight o'clock? Be sure to practise your piano before you come.'

32

Ari Thór was now convinced that Hávardur's macabre message was unrelated to Unnur's death. However, he kept replaying their conversation in his mind and had to admit that there had been something odd and intriguing about it. The elderly man had seemed so sure that he had witnessed a murder. The determination on his face, those chilling words scrawled repeatedly on the wall ... and who was the mysterious Finnbogi he had spoken about?

All this left Ari Thór feeling uneasy. Maybe there was some truth to Hávardur's assertions, he thought. Perhaps a terrible crime had been committed long ago. Something that had faded into the darkness of memory. But now was not the time to dig up the past. Ari Thór couldn't afford to let himself be sidetracked.

He decided to pay Hersir a visit to let him know how the conversation with Hávardur had gone. It was the doctor's wife who opened the door.

'Oh, hello, Ari Thór. To what do I owe the pleasure?' Rósa greeted him with a smile. In one hand she held a demitasse of steaming espresso. The rich aroma wafted straight to Ari Thór's nostrils.

Somewhere in the background, a radio was playing old Icelandic folk songs.

'Hersir isn't here,' Rósa volunteered, before Ari Thór had time to ask.

'Ah, I see. I just wanted to…'

'Oh, do come in, won't you? I'll make you a coffee. He's at work at the moment,' she explained.

'That's strange. I just came from the nursing home and I didn't see him.'

'He's at the hospital, not the home. He still does the odd shift here and there, when they need him. He shouldn't be too long, actually. Would you like me to give him a call?'

'No, it's all right. It's nothing urgent. I'd love a coffee, though, thanks. It's late in the day, but it'll keep me going.'

'Espresso?'

He nodded.

'So, what do you think of our little renovation project? The care home, I mean,' Rósa asked, once they were sitting down.

'I'm very impressed,' Ari Thór replied. 'The old schoolhouse had been neglected for years, so it must have been a big job.'

'You can say that again. It's been Hersir's dream to resurrect that place, and he's put everything into making it happen. If things go well, it will be quite a profitable venture, even though we've had a bit of a bumpy start. Residents are still only trickling in, but at least we've signed an agreement now with the authorities. I think the worst is behind us. We're looking forward to hiring more staff and giving something back to the community.' She took a sip of her coffee. 'I'm glad I've been able to do my part, albeit indirectly. To have helped him make his dream a reality – or at least save us from bankruptcy.'

'Was there a real risk of that happening, then?'

Rósa thought for a moment, considering her words.

'To be perfectly honest, at one point it was just a matter of days. It's no small feat to undertake a project of this scale, you know, especially in a small community like ours.'

'But all's well that ends well, right?'

'You could say that,' she acknowledged with a smile.

'Besides having a hand in the nursing home, do you do anything else for a living?' Ari Thór asked.

'I run a small art gallery in town, at least for now. I studied art, and I've always worked in that field. As you might already know, my mother's side of the family hails from this part of the country. But until now, I'd never lived in Siglufjörður myself. My husband's always liked the place, so we used to come and visit quite regularly. He's really into skiing and being in the great outdoors. And for me, well, it's an artist's paradise. There's so much culture here. I'm a writer, too, as it happens. I've written a book about art history, and I'm hoping teachers will start to use it with their students. Siglufjörður is so calm and peaceful, it's an ideal place for writers and artists to work.'

'Perhaps you know Gudjón Helgason?' Ari Thór asked.

'I certainly do. He's one of the most exciting artists we've been fortunate to have in residence, if you ask me. Are you a fan? Do you have one of his pieces?'

Ari Thór shook his head, amused that she would think that.

'I'm not what you'd call an art collector. Our paths have crossed recently, that's all. He was wandering the streets in the dead of night.'

Rósa chuckled. 'Oh, that's just like him. He's not like…'

Not like normal people, Ari Thór thought to himself.

'Let's just say he's a bit different,' Rósa explained.

'But let me guess: he wouldn't hurt a fly?' Ari Thór wasn't sure that was appropriate, but he said it anyway.

'Certainly not. Has he done something wrong?'

'No, not that I'm aware of,' Ari Thór replied, without elaborating.

Rósa put her espresso cup down and glanced at it to make

sure she had sipped every last drop, then looked up to meet Ari Thór's gaze. 'I'm sorry to have wasted your time. You never quite know when to expect Hersir. He's not the most punctual man in the world. What did you want to talk to him about? Maybe I can help?'

'I doubt it. But like I said, it can wait. It's about one of his residents at the nursing home.'

'Oh, really?'

Despite his initial hesitation, Ari Thór decided he might as well share his concerns.

'His name is Hávardur.'

'Hávardur?' She clearly recognised the name.

'I imagine you know who I'm talking about?' Ari Thór asked.

'Of course,' Rósa replied. 'I've spent quite a bit of time with him over at the nursing home. He has his good days.'

'And some not-so-good days, I gather.'

Rósa nodded.

'Perhaps you can tell me a bit about him, then. Maybe he's talked to you about his life when he was younger?' Ari Thór was clutching at straws now.

'Hmm … I'm not sure I can. My parents would have been better placed to tell you about his background. They knew everyone here. He's from Siglufjörður, I know that. He has a son in town, and I think he worked at the library for the better part of his life. It's a shame my late aunt ended up losing her faculties, because she was at the home too, and they might have got to know each other before she passed away. I'm sure she would have had plenty of stories to tell me about him. Their generation is slowly disappearing. And the rest of us aren't exactly going to great lengths to preserve the past.'

'I'd be tempted to agree.'

'We get so caught up in our daily lives, don't we?' Rósa smiled.

'You've done a nice job with this place too,' Ari Thór said, keeping the conversation flowing.

'Thanks. We still have a house in Reykjavík too. It's nice to know we have somewhere to retreat to if things here don't work out the way we're hoping. At the moment, though, I'm still quite optimistic. A lot of the time, things work themselves out somehow, as if God's smiling down on us.'

Ari Thór had long since stopped believing in the Almighty. Losing both parents as a teenager had certainly tainted his belief, and the theology studies he had then undertaken and failed to complete had done nothing to restore his faith. That said, he did feel that the church played a more important role in his life here – in this small, remote community where the pastor bandaged the wounds of all and sundry – than it had back in Reykjavík. Siglufjörður had historically depended on the fishing industry for its survival, and many whose loved ones went to sea must have found comfort in the belief that God would protect them.

Ari Thór had finished his coffee but was still nursing his espresso cup. 'I'd better get going, but…'

He left his words hanging, and Rósa understood this to mean that he would still like to speak with Hersir.

'Would you like me to phone him? He's always available if there's an issue with any of his patients or residents. Even though they're always in good hands with the carers – they look after them day in, day out. Ugla's one. Do you know her?'

'We're acquainted,' Ari Thór replied, being intentionally vague. He stood up.

'Would you like me to give Hersir a message when he gets home?' Rósa asked.

'Certainly. I just wanted to let him know that I'd spoken to Hávardur and … perhaps ask him a few questions about someone by the name of Finnbogi.'

'Finnbogi? Who's that?'

'That's what I'm trying to find out…'

'What's happened with Hávardur? Has he done something wrong? The poor man.'

Ari Thór released a nervous laugh. 'No, not at all. He just scribbled something quite concerning on the wall of his room. Ugla told me about it, because it happened shortly after the body of a teenage girl was discovered.'

This seemed to pique Rósa's curiosity. 'Oh, really? What did he write? Was it something…?'

She left her question unfinished, and Ari Thór wondered what she was going to ask.

He shrugged. 'Nothing that really made sense, but I don't want to neglect any leads.'

Still seated, Rósa was staring at him now, looking as if she was determined that he wouldn't leave without telling her everything. She picked up her empty espresso cup and started toying with it nervously.

He figured he had nothing to hide. '"She was murdered". That's what he wrote.'

'She was … *what?*' Rósa echoed, the colour suddenly draining from her face. 'Sorry, what did you say?'

'"She was murdered". He scrawled those words repeatedly all over his wall. In red capital letters. It was quite unsettling for Ugla to discover that, so I'm not surprised she got in touch with me. I'll be damned if I know what Hávardur was referring to, anyway. It could be something he saw on TV, or an old memory that's resurfaced for some reason.'

Rósa had stopped listening to him. She put her demitasse down again with a clatter, and it made Ari Thór jump.

'I'm sorry, I'm tired,' she said, with a quiver in her voice.

'There's no need to apologise,' Ari Thór replied.

Now Rósa got to her feet. 'Hersir must have been delayed. I'm sorry I couldn't help. I'll ask him to give you a call.'

She was clearly keen to get rid of Ari Thór now. But he was in no hurry to leave. Not now that his senses were fully on alert.

Rósa's attitude had shifted dramatically as soon as he said those three words: *She was murdered.*

Could Rósa know the secret behind their meaning? Or did she know something about Unnur?

'Do you know Hávardur well?' Ari Thór pressed. 'Or did you, before his health began to decline?'

'No. Not in the slightest,' she replied, not without irritation.

Ari Thór was observing her reactions. Her eyes darted around the room, avoiding his gaze, and her voice was still shaking.

'What about that message – "she was murdered"?' he continued. 'What do you think that could mean?'

'What do I think? How am I supposed to know?' she snapped. A split second later, she pulled herself together. 'I'm sorry, I didn't mean to lose my cool, but … obviously I don't know what he was trying to say. It must be something to do with his cognitive decline, I imagine. Wouldn't you agree?'

'That's what I'd be inclined to think,' Ari Thór replied.

Rósa forced a smile and accompanied him to the door.

'I trust you'll give Hersir the message?' Ari Thór insisted.

'Yes, of course.'

He said goodbye and stepped out into the whirling white beginnings of the blizzard.

33

As soon as Ari Thór got home, he stretched out on the sofa for a rest. He was fast asleep when his phone rang. It was past ten at night on Easter Sunday, and the call was from a number he didn't recognise. This didn't bode well.

The blizzard was raging outside now. The wind was blowing so hard, it was making the old wooden house creak. Kristín had made the right decision to leave town before all hell broke loose.

'Hello?' he answered, sitting up and rubbing his eyes.

'It's Svavar,' the man at the other end of the line barked, clearly not bothering with any pleasantries.

It took a few seconds for Ari Thór to wake up and remember who the man was. Unnur's father had not been particularly pleasant when they had spoken at the breakfast table in the hotel. It looked like this conversation was taking just as unpleasant a turn before it even started.

'What the hell is this, Ari Thór? Can't you do your job properly?' Svavar hissed.

Ari Thór thought he could detect the hint of an American accent in the man's voice. He hadn't picked up on that the other day.

'I'm sorry, Svavar, but this is completely out of line. It's not just the weekend, it's a public holiday, and you have no right to phone me at this time of night and speak to me so disrespectfully—'

Svavar cut him off mid-sentence. 'Now you listen to me. My daughter was murdered, so I have every right to disturb you whenever the hell I like, do you hear me? You're not doing your job! When are you going to arrest that guy? What are you waiting for?'

'Who are you talking about?'

'Seriously? Bjarki, you clown!'

'Bjarki? What makes you think I should arrest him?'

'He was her teacher!'

'Whose teacher?'

'My daughter's, for God's sake!' Svavar yelled.

Ari Thór didn't let the man's aggression get to him, but he was taken aback by the information.

'What do you mean, he was her teacher?'

Bjarki hadn't said a word about this to Ari Thór. He hadn't even mentioned that he knew who Unnur was.

'He was her history teacher. Or so I've been told. Obviously you weren't aware of that,' Svavar spat. 'I've been doing some digging of my own, you see. There's something about that building where she was found lying in the street, so I've gathered as much information as I can about the people who live there. That's exactly what you should have done. This investigation is a disgrace. It's unbelievable what a shoddy job you've done. So are you going to arrest the guy, or do I have to march over to his place and give him a piece of my mind?'

'Just calm down, Svavar. Let me be clear. Bjarki was in Reykjavík when your daughter died. I would urge you not to do something you might regret.'

'No, no of course not. I just want you to arrest the guy and bring him in for questioning,' Svavar explained, his temper seeming to subside.

'I'll be the judge of that,' Ari Thór replied. 'Thank you for passing this information along. I have to go now. I'll be in touch tomorrow.'

'All right, then. Thanks.' Svavar sounded remarkably subdued now. Perhaps he had just needed to get his frustration off his chest.

Ari Thór collapsed on the sofa again and closed his eyes. He had decided to sleep in the living room, with the lights on, and let the whistling of the wind outside lull him to sleep. Upstairs, in a bedroom plunged into darkness, he was worried that solitude would get the better of him.

Bjarki could wait until the morning.

EASTER MONDAY

34

Bjarki.

Ari Thór woke with a shiver, thinking about the historian and his connection to the young woman who died. It hadn't been the most comfortable night's sleep on the sofa. And dawn had done nothing to calm the raging blizzard outside.

Jenný was standing in front of Bjarki's building. Maybe she saw him coming or going.

If Bjarki had been Unnur's history teacher, he would likely have been Jenný's too, Ari Thór realised. If she had seen him, she would almost certainly have recognised him.

Obviously, she could just have well have caught a glimpse of Jóhann or Jónína, or someone else, for that matter, but the Bjarki connection was troubling, to say the least. It was time to determine whether his alibi was as solid as it seemed.

Ignoring the fact that it was barely eight in the morning, Ari Thór called Ögmundur and asked him to check whether Bjarki was actually in Reykjavík at the time of Unnur's death, as he had claimed. Until now, Ari Thór had had no reason to doubt the man's word. It wasn't a habit of his to ask everyone he spoke to in the course of investigating a suspected suicide to confirm their whereabouts.

An hour later, his junior officer called back. After several phone calls to Reykjavík – which had met with a lukewarm reception, given the early hour – Ögmundur had established that Bjarki was telling the truth.

'He gave a presentation that afternoon, and he spent the whole evening drinking and socialising. There's no way he could have got back to Siglufjörður in time to be at the scene. Plus, Ari Thór, you know as well as I do, that girl wasn't murdered.'

Ögmundur then seemed keen to change the subject: 'Have you seen the weather? It's getting really bad. They said on the forecast we should expect the power to go out. The snow's coming down thick and fast, and the wind is howling. I've never seen anything like it.'

What a big-city wimp, Ari Thór thought. It was hard for him to believe now that he had once said the same thing about the harsh winter storms in Siglufjörður.

❄

Bundled up in his parka, with a woolly hat pulled down to his eyes under his hood, Ari Thór set out on foot and, with some difficulty, made slow headway against the wind. He had always enjoyed braving the elements. There was something about defying the forces of nature that made him feel alive. The wind had blown the overnight snowfall into drifts, making the roads impassable. Visibility was still close to zero.

One step at a time, Ari Thór trudged his way up the hill to the house where Jenný lived with her parents. Her mother looked surprised to find him knocking at the door. No one expected visitors in weather as bad as this.

He introduced himself, almost having to shout to make himself heard over the howling of the wind. 'I'm sorry to disturb you. I just wanted to ask your daughter some questions about Unnur.'

'Come in, come in!' Jenný's mother cried. 'Don't just stand there, you'll catch your death.'

Once Ari Thór had stepped into the hallway and closed the door behind him, she hastened to say: 'You can certainly talk to her. But she's still feeling the shock of what happened. It's perfectly understandable, of course. Suicide in a small community is never an easy thing for any of us to come to terms with.'

'That's putting it mildly. I can come back later, if you'd rather,' Ari Thór offered, albeit begrudgingly. He was keen to get to the bottom of things and put this matter to rest.

'No, it's all right,' Jenný's mother replied. 'She's upstairs in her room. I'll let her know you're here. Do you mind having me present when you talk to her, though? Her father's not here at the moment. He volunteers with the search-and-rescue team, and he's out on an emergency call. They've gone to rescue a couple whose car's got stuck in the snow on the edge of town.'

'Why don't we let Jenný decide?' Ari Thór suggested, turning to look at the teenager who had appeared at the bottom of the stairs without her mother having to call her. She seemed to have heard at least part of their conversation.

'Don't worry, Mum. I'll talk to him on my own,' Jenný said.

Then she looked Ari Thór in the eye. 'Can we do this at the police station?'

'Don't be silly, sweetheart. It's out of the question for you to leave the house in this weather,' her mother objected.

Jenný didn't bother to reply. She simply pulled on her coat and boots, and was out the door in a flash. It was all Ari Thór could do to catch up with her. They walked for a while without a word, before Ari Thór broke the silence.

'I think I know who you saw, Jenný.'

He ushered her into some semblance of shelter behind a wall. The wind was whirling around in all directions, whipping at their faces and making it hard to hear themselves.

'It was Bjarki, wasn't it?' he asked. It came out more like a statement than a question.

'I…' she stammered, her face suddenly veiled in darkness. 'Yes, it was him that I saw. How did you…?'

'It doesn't matter how I knew it was him. You just have to tell me the truth now, Jenný.'

'I don't know what to say. I'm not sure I'm comfortable telling you about this … I don't want to get into trouble, you know. I don't want my parents to find out. I'd be mortified if they did. No one else can know,' she insisted.

The snow was coming down relentlessly.

'I'll do my best to be discreet, Jenný, I can promise you that. But if Bjarki did anything to hurt Unnur, I have to take action.'

'But I won't have to get mixed up in that, will I?'

'Not necessarily, no.'

'Do you think he did something to her? Do you think he pushed her off that balcony?' Jenný asked.

'What do you think?'

She thought for a moment.

'No, I don't see how … no one could…'

'People are capable of anything, Jenný. Even the things you least suspect. Never forget that. But I sincerely hope you're right. What happened with Bjarki?'

Jenný stood in silence for a long while, narrowing her eyes

against the blizzard raging around them. Ari Thór was trying to be patient and give her the time and space she needed, even though the bitter cold was becoming unbearable.

'Can we talk about this indoors?' Jenný eventually asked, in a shaky voice.

'Absolutely. Let's go.' Ari Thór led the way, striding purposefully through the snow.

They advanced in silence, making quick progress through the deserted streets, jumping over or trudging through the many snowdrifts that blocked the pavement. Ari Thór couldn't wait to be out of the wind and the cold. It seemed that Jenný was ready to tell him the truth at last, and he was eager to hear what she had to say. The sooner they were warm and dry indoors, the better. Experience had taught him that time was of the essence when a reluctant witness was suddenly willing to talk.

They arrived at the police station to find the front door locked. Ögmundur should have been there, on duty, but he had obviously decided he'd rather stay at home than brave the storm. He would have some explaining to do.

Ari Thór unlocked the door and held it open for Jenný to go inside. He closed the door behind them and glanced at her. She looked terribly uncomfortable.

'Let's sit in the kitchen,' Ari Thór said, thinking that would be a more informal environment than his office. 'Would you like a coffee?' he suggested, trying to make her feel more at ease.

'I'd love one, thanks,' she replied, taking a seat. 'Black, no sugar.'

Ari Thór took off his parka and hung it on a hook on the wall. It was a black coat, but right now it was covered in such a thick layer of snow it looked white. Jenný kept her own coat on. She sat in silence, staring at the table as Ari Thór fired up the new espresso machine.

He figured that if he was going to drink coffee, he might as well drink the good stuff, so he had decided to purchase a decent machine for the station. But he didn't have the heart to get rid of the old Italian stovetop espresso maker that had initiated him into the pleasures of drinking good, strong coffee. Not yet.

'He doesn't look like it...' Jenný murmured, after a few warming sips of her coffee. 'You'd never suspect it, but he's such a filthy pervert.'

'What are you insinuating, Jenný?'

'I know I'm not the first girl at school he's tried to put the moves on,' she blurted.

Ari Thór had begun to harbour some suspicions about Bjarki, but it was eye-opening to hear them confirmed by a young woman the same age as Unnur.

It turned Ari Thór's stomach now to think that he had considered befriending Bjarki. He now saw the man who had seemed so courteous and respectable in a whole new light, and it disturbed him.

'It's all right, Jenný. You can tell me everything.'

'Our history teacher was away for a couple of months last autumn, and Bjarki replaced him. It started pretty much right away. He was always careful not to go too far, and to keep up appearances. I got the impression he had a lot of experience doing that sort of thing. He never really spoke to me in class, but as soon as we were outside the classroom, he would take advantage of the slightest opportunity to talk to me. He assigned the class a written project to work on at home that term, and because I was really into history, he offered to help me with some research after school. So I'd get a better mark on my essay, he said. Anyway, I met him once after school and nothing happened, but when we met up again the following week, he was more insistent. He knew exactly what he was doing.'

'And so did things … escalate?' Ari Thór asked.

Jenný considered her words in silence. When she spoke again, it was barely a whisper.

'I don't understand how, really. I thought he was nice, and I guess I was scared to say no, so…'

Ari Thór spoke up so that she wouldn't feel she had to finish her sentence.

'You don't have to feel guilty or justify anything, Jenný. And you certainly don't have to tell me any more than you want to, if it makes you feel uncomfortable. All I need to know, is if he subjected Unnur to the same sort of thing, and how far he might have taken things with her.'

Jenný sprang to her feet. Not to leave, but as if standing would help her to take a deep breath and free her conscience.

'Take your time,' Ari Thór coaxed.

'It went on for about a month,' Jenný explained. Her voice was wavering like a timid flame. 'I didn't say a word to anyone. I was too ashamed. I regretted letting him do what he did. I eventually stopped responding to his texts and he left me alone. It was really embarrassing to still see him at school, but I put on a brave face. He was just so cold to me, though. He didn't seem the slightest bit bothered by what had happened. I don't know … I don't know why I didn't say anything, but … maybe Unnur would still be alive if…'

'Jenný,' Ari Thór said softly, weighing his words carefully. 'According to our information, Bjarki was in Reykjavík at the time Unnur died. Do you have reason to believe that may not be true? That he might have wanted to hurt her?'

The teenager's lips curled downward into a grimace so pained it tugged at Ari Thór's heart.

'Hurt her? That's one way to put it,' she hissed, throwing daggers at him with her eyes. 'I don't know if he killed her. I don't know if he actually pushed her off that balcony. It's up to you to figure that out. But if he did to her what he did to me, then of course he hurt her!' she cried. 'I should have told someone. I should have reported him. But I didn't. I just tried to forget it had ever happened. I thought he would just move away, and it would all be better. I wasn't going to stick around in this town for much longer myself, if I could help it. And he was supposed to be going to Canada in September. I was hoping he would go over there and never set foot here again.'

'Are you saying he...?'

'That's exactly what I'm saying!' she insisted. 'It's no way for anyone to behave, let alone a teacher. He abused his position. He was ... threatening. I felt like he tried to intimidate me when I told him I didn't want to do it anymore. He stopped hassling me in the end, but what if he just went on to prey on another poor, innocent girl instead? Like Unnur...'

'What makes you think he might have preyed on Unnur?'

'That's where she died, wasn't it? Right in front of his place. She fell from his balcony! What more proof do you need?'

Ari Thór nodded.

'Of all the buildings in town, do you really think she picked that one at random?' Jenný added. 'Plus, she wasn't exactly popular at school. She was the shy, sensitive type. Precisely the kind of girl bastards like him target. She had no friends to confide in ... no one she could trust. Now do you see what I'm saying?'

'I understand, Jenný.'

'Do you remember, when I came to see you the other day, I told you Unnur was far too naive and innocent? Well, now you know what I meant by that. I wanted to tell you everything right then, but I just couldn't bring myself to say the words. I didn't have the strength.'

Ari Thór nodded sympathetically.

'Did he ever take you up to his flat?' he asked.

'Twice. Both times were at night. We went in through the back door, so the downstairs neighbours wouldn't see us.' She frowned. 'What was it that he said about them? Oh, yes, they were just a couple of old nosy gossips, that's what he said.'

Jenný had been standing the whole time, and the snow on her jacket had melted and dripped onto the floor, forming a puddle around her feet.

Ari Thór saw no reason to draw out the conversation any further. His priority now was to pay Bjarki another visit. 'Thank you very much for telling me this, Jenný,' he said. 'I think this will be enough information, at least for now.'

'You're … you're not going to involve me in all this, are you?' she asked timidly, with downcast eyes.

'I don't think that will be necessary,' Ari Thór replied. 'I will have to question Bjarki, of course, based on what you've told me, but you can count on my discretion. He's not teaching at your high school anymore, I presume?'

'No,' she murmured. 'I didn't mean to … I should have said something sooner. I really hope he didn't get his filthy paws on Unnur…'

'But you suspect he might have?'

She nodded.

'Leave it with me,' Ari Thór reassured her. 'Don't worry. I'll let you know if there are any developments.'

He walked her to the door. 'Would you like me to walk home with you?' he offered.

'No, I'll be all right. But there is one more thing. He gave me a mobile phone when we were … seeing each other. Just a cheap, old thing.'

'Why?' Ari Thór asked.

'So we could text each other things that would stay between us, as he put it. Without anyone knowing, more like. Anyway, I took it, and I used it – I don't really know why. It seems so obvious to me now that it was all part of his plan.'

'Do you still have it?'

She shook her head. 'He asked me to give it back. I had no desire at all to keep his dirty messages, so I didn't take much convincing. Maybe I did the wrong thing. I should have kept it, shouldn't I?'

'No, it wouldn't have made a difference,' Ari Thór lied.

He would have liked to get his hands on that phone. It was evidence. Tangible proof of Jenný's revelations. Without that phone, he would have to knock at Bjarki's door armed with nothing more than Jenný's word – and hope that it would be enough to tease the truth out of the man.

35

'Salvör, do you know if Unnur had another phone?'

Ari Thór was standing at her door, wincing as the blowing snow whipped at his face.

'Another phone? What do you mean?'

'I'm wondering if she had a second mobile phone.'

'I don't think so. I doubt it. If she did, she would have told me. Why would she want another phone? She was perfectly happy with her smartphone. Her father bought it for her in America. Why do you want to know?'

'If she did, where do you think she would have kept it?'

Ari Thór suddenly remembered the break-in Salvör had reported. He went over the timeline of events in his mind, and there was no doubt about it: Bjarki was in Siglufjörður when it happened. He had told Ari Thór himself that he had cut short his trip to Reykjavík. To get rid of the evidence, perhaps?

'Come in out of the cold, won't you? I'll have a look,' Salvör said, without asking any more questions.

Ari Thór sat at the kitchen table and waited patiently while she went upstairs. There was an eerie sense of calm in the air. By all appearances, the house was perfectly in order. But everything in it was invisibly tainted by grief.

Ari Thór allowed his thoughts to wander for a moment. He had to gather as much evidence as possible before confronting Bjarki. But he couldn't stop thinking about his visit to Rósa, the doctor's wife, and her suspicious reaction when he told her about Hávardur's chilling message. He decided to take advantage of these few minutes to himself to give Ugla a call.

She sounded surprised to hear from him. 'Ari Thór? Is everything all right? Aren't we supposed to be seeing each other tonight?'

'Yes, of course. I'm coming to your place at eight, as promised. I just wanted to ask you a question.'

'Are you sure everything's all right?' she asked.

'Absolutely. Let's just say I'm too busy to be bored.'

'You need to slow down a bit, Ari Thór. Why don't you let your colleague…?'

'Ögmundur?'

'Yes. Let him pick up some of the slack. Remember to look after yourself.'

'I'll think about it,' he replied stubbornly. 'Listen, I was talking to Hersir's wife last night…'

'Oh, yes, Rósa. I like her. Such a sweet lady.'

'I'm sure she is, but when I told her about Hávardur, her reaction was quite eye-opening.'

'What do you mean?'

'It's hard to say exactly. But she seemed devastated. Not just shocked – because those words would shock anyone, I think – but devastated.'

'Why?'

'I have no idea. Did she know Unnur?'

'I don't know,' Ugla replied.

'I gather she doesn't know Hávardur very well either, does she?' Ari Thór continued.

'No, I don't think she does…'

'It struck me as suspicious, but maybe I'm reading too much into it…'

'Maybe she was afraid.'

'Afraid?' Ari Thór was surprised by Ugla's suggestion.

'Of what it would mean for Hersir and the nursing home

– if they were to be connected with a suspicious death. After all the time and money they've invested in their project, it's understandable that she'd be worried about their reputation. You have to admit, it doesn't look good for one of their residents to be scrawling "she was murdered" all over his wall…'

Ari Thór thought about the implications of what Ugla had said. Before he had time to reply, she added: 'Obviously I haven't told anyone else about this, only you. I'm bound by confidentiality, as you know. So she doesn't have to worry about me betraying any secrets.'

Ari Thór had his doubts about that theory, but he decided to keep them to himself. Ugla's explanation seemed a bit too simplistic and superficial. There must be something else, something more deep-rooted, behind Rósa's reaction. And he wouldn't rest until he knew what that was.

He thanked Ugla and hung up just as Salvör reappeared at the foot of the stairs.

She seemed disappointed. 'I looked, but I couldn't find a phone, Ari Thór.'

'Is there anywhere else it might be, somewhere you might not have thought to check? A favourite hiding place from her childhood, perhaps?'

Salvör's face lit up with a flash of recollection. 'Yes … she did used to have a little hiding place.'

'Where?'

'In the cellar. There was a little nook where she liked to tuck herself away to play with the little knick-knacks she collected. It was an alcove behind the rack of old milk bottles we keep down there. I don't think she knew…'

'She didn't know that you knew about her little hiding place?' Ari Thór guessed.

'That's right.'

Salvör led him to the cellar door, and he followed her down a rickety staircase. The ceiling was so low, they both had to stoop. The dark, damp crawl space would have been a creepy place at the best of times, but with the blizzard raging outside, and the snow piling up in drifts, it seemed more like a tomb.

'There's a light switch here somewhere,' Salvör said, feeling her way along the wall in the dark.

A second later, a bare lightbulb hanging from the ceiling flickered to life.

'There's the rack of bottles,' she said, pointing to her left.

She crouched down and shuffled her way over to the far corner of the cellar, while Ari Thór watched. The old glass milk bottles – relics of a bygone era – clinked as she moved the rack to one side, revealing a little nook set into the cellar wall.

'There's something here,' she said, reaching forward to pull a small object out from the shadows.

Salvör could barely believe her eyes. She turned to Ari Thór to show him what she had found. It was a mobile phone, as he had suspected. In the faint light of the old, damp cellar, her face betrayed a mix of emotions – surprise, disappointment and fear.

36

In the course of his short career, Ari Thór had experienced many events he was unlikely to forget. And the reasons for that fact were rarely positive.

Finding the lifeless body of a teenage girl at the beginning of the long Easter weekend was one of these moments that would forever haunt him. As was the discovery of the messages that lurked on her secret phone.

Back at the police station, Ari Thór had found a charger that fit the device, plugged it in at his desk and, once the battery had come back to life, scrolled through the contents.

There were no photos, only texts. But they told a story that filled Ari Thór with horror.

The story of a young woman full of promise and potential who had made the terrible decision to take her own life.

And now, he had to go and see her mother to try and put the disturbing truth into words.

37

As Ari Thór left the police station, the streets were thick with drifting snow and the wind was howling even stronger than before. Heading out into the storm, he felt like he was alone in the world. He was almost certainly alone in the streets of Siglufjörður, though it was hard to tell in the eerie, swirling whiteness.

The ringing of his phone, somewhere deep in the pockets of his parka, stopped him in his tracks, before he had taken more than a few steps. He swiftly turned around and took refuge inside the station entrance to answer the call.

'This is Thormódur Hávardarson,' the caller announced. 'I saw I had a missed call from this number.'

It had completely slipped Ari Thór's mind that he had tried to get in touch with Hávardur's son. He had wanted to ask him about the mysterious Finnbogi his father had mentioned. After the revelations in the Unnur case, that phone call was now less of a priority. He was reluctant to keep Salvör waiting, but it couldn't hurt to take a few moments to speak with Thormódur.

'Hello Thormódur, this is Inspector Ari Thór Arason. Thanks for returning my call.'

'No problem. Sorry I didn't pick up before. I barely even use my phone. I always seem to leave it lying around somewhere with the ringer off.'

'Just a quick question…' Ari Thór said. 'Does the name Finnbogi mean anything to you? Do you know anyone with that name?'

'Finnbogi? No, I don't think so. Unless…'

Whatever Thormódur was thinking, he didn't voice it.

'What about your father? Maybe he knew a Finnbogi?' Ari Thór suggested.

'I'm not sure … now that you mention it, the name does ring a bell. I don't know why. I can't quite place it.'

'Well, please call me back if anything comes back to you.' Ari Thór was getting anxious to be on his way.

'Yes, I certainly will.'

Ari Thór ended the call and set out for Salvör's house on Grundargata, advancing through the whiteout as quickly as the conditions would allow.

Unnur's mother hurried to open the door as he approached, her face ravaged with concern. She motioned for him to sit down in the dimly lit living room.

He was just about to tell her what he had uncovered, when the power went out, plunging the room into darkness for a few long seconds before the lights flickered back on. A chill ran down Ari Thór's spine, even though he hadn't taken off his parka.

'I've been through the contents of the phone, Salvör. You said you never saw your daughter using it?'

'No. I don't get it. She had the latest smartphone, so why would she want to use that old-fashioned thing?'

Ari Thór glanced out the window, trying to shake the sudden sense of claustrophobia that had closed in around him. It was a familiar feeling, one that he had experienced a lot during his first winter in Siglufjörður.

'She was using it to exchange text messages with a man,' Ari Thór said. 'I'll need to keep it for a while so we can examine it more thoroughly. I can't say too much right now, but their last few texts were rather concerning.'

He paused, not quite sure how to phrase what he had to tell the victim's mother. He was almost hoping that Salvör was going to chime in and say something first, but she remained silent and motionless, frozen on the edge of her seat, staring at him, waiting to hear what he had to say.

'Salvör, everything seems to suggest that they were in an intimate relationship, and that it didn't end well.'

She remained silent, letting his words sink in.

'She broke it off – or at least she tried to – but he … he didn't want to let her go.'

'Who was it? What did he do?' Salvör stammered.

Ari Thór wanted to get this over and done with as quickly as possible. He had a duty to convey this information, no matter how devastating the consequences.

'He was threatening her. He said he would post photos of her online if she left him.'

'Photos?' Salvör looked puzzled at first. Before it dawned on her what Ari Thór was saying. 'Do you know who it was?' she asked.

'The number she was texting is unregistered – like the phone she was using – but she mentioned the man's name in some of her messages. His name is Bjarki.'

'Bjarki?'

'He was a replacement teacher at her school. And he lives in the building where…'

'Bjarki? The historian?' Salvör all but shouted the words. For a second, the echo seemed to hang in the air.

Ari Thór nodded.

'They were … *together*?'

'So it seems.'

'And … you think he pushed her?' she faltered, choking back a tear.

'I don't think so. Not physically, at least. He was in Reykjavík when it happened.'

'But you're going to arrest him, aren't you?'
'Let's just say I'm going to have words with him.'

Ari Thór was on his way over to Bjarki's flat when he heard the faint sound of his phone ringing deep in his pocket. Fortunately he was just a few steps away from the bakery, so he darted inside to take shelter from the blizzard and answer the call. The young man behind the counter was alarmed to see him come in the door completely covered in snow. The place was deserted. It was a wonder it wasn't closed because of the storm.

Ari Thór sat at a table by the window, reaching into his pocket to retrieve his phone. The visibility in the whiteout behind the glass was so poor, he could barely see the street through the blowing snow.

'Hi, Ari Thór. It's Thormódur again. I've just remembered who Finnbogi is.'

'I'm all ears.'

'He was our family doctor when I was growing up. He practised in Sigló for many years. He and Dad were good friends. They were both members of the Lions and the Freemasons.'

'Is he still alive?'

'No, he died a long time ago.'

'Thanks, Thormódur. I'm sure that will help.' That was all Ari Thór needed to know for now. It was time for him to get going.

Ari Thór had made plans to meet up with Ugla that evening, but he was reluctant to bother her in the meantime. He didn't want to seem too keen and risk upsetting the fine balance of the relationship they were rebuilding. He was looking forward to seeing her again and it was a refreshing feeling. Things seemed to be off to a promising start. But he knew only too well how fragile new beginnings could be. The first time there had been a spark between them, it had fizzled out and Ugla had shut the door on him for years. Now she was opening that door again, just enough to let a chink of light shine into his life.

Thormódur's call had made Ari Thór rethink his plan to confront Bjarki. That could wait until later. First, he would pay Hávardur a visit at the care home. He left the deserted bakery and set out once more into the storm, head low and shoulders hunched. The hill seemed steeper than ever, but before long he was pushing open the door to the old schoolhouse. He was pleasantly surprised to cross paths with Ugla in the corridor as he was dusting himself off.

'Ari Thór? What are you doing here? You look like the abominable snowman,' she teased.

'I just wanted to have a quick word with you – and Hávardur,' he replied.

'It's hellish out there. I've never seen a blizzard like it. The lights keep flickering on and off. I spoke to Hersir on the phone earlier, and he said he was worried there was going to be a blackout.'

'I wouldn't be surprised,' Ari Thór admitted. 'They said on

the news that might happen. Listen, do you remember that Hávardur mentioned someone named Finnbogi the other day?'

Ugla nodded.

'He was his former doctor,' Ari Thór explained. 'I might be wrong, but I have an idea what—'

Before he could finish, Ugla interrupted him. 'You know what? I'm glad you came by. I was going to mention it tonight, but something struck me after our conversation about Hersir's wife.'

'Go on,' Ari Thór urged.

'I don't know if it's important, but Rósa spent a lot of time with Hávardur earlier this winter…'

'What do you mean, a lot of time?'

'You know how there are two beds in each room? Well, Rósa's aunt was in the other bed in Hávardur's room. She was very elderly, and her mind wasn't what it used to be. She was our first resident here at the home. She was born and raised in Siglufjörður, and her husband was the biggest shipowner in the area.'

'When did she die?'

'About two months ago. Since then, Hávardur's had the room to himself, as I'm sure you'll have noticed. Not for long though, I imagine, because Hersir's hoping to bring in more residents.'

Ari Thór considered his words carefully before asking his next question.

'About Rósa's aunt's death … was it sudden?'

'Sudden? How so?'

'Did you see it coming?'

Was it suspicious? That was the question he really wanted to ask. Hávardur had scrawled 'she was murdered' all over his wall two months after the death of the woman who had shared his room at the care home. And he had done so at a time when chins were wagging all over town about another female's death. Maybe Ari Thór was imagining things, but…

Ugla didn't answer his question right away.

'It did seem quite sudden, yes. I'm not a doctor, of course, but she seemed to be in good health to me. Well, it's all relative, I suppose. She never used to say much, and she'd been bedridden for ages, but she was still going strong, I thought.'

'What did Hersir say when she died?'

'He didn't seem particularly surprised.' She hesitated, then continued with a slight tremor in her voice: 'It sounds cruel to say it, but … it's almost as if her death was convenient.'

'What do you mean?' Ari Thór asked. The picture he had been piecing together in his mind was gradually becoming clearer.

'Well, she was her only heir.'

'Who?' Ari Thór already knew the answer, but he wanted her to say the woman's name.

'Rósa. Her aunt didn't have children of her own. And she made no secret of the fact that Rósa stood to inherit every penny the old woman had to her name. If you ask me, she and Hersir are probably quite comfortably off now. With all the money from the fishing quotas she'd been sitting on.'

Ari Thór stood in silence as the missing pieces of the puzzle slotted into place in his mind.

'That's very interesting,' he eventually said.

He couldn't stop thinking about the message the elderly man had scrawled on the wall of his room in red capital letters. In light of Ugla's revelation, those three words seemed to take on a chilling new meaning. *She was murdered.*

'Ari Thór…' Ugla murmured. 'You don't think that … no, of course not…'

He waited for her to find the right words.

'Do you think they might have … you know…?'

'They? Do you think they both had a hand in it?'

Now Ugla played devil's advocate. 'No, no way. I've known Hersir for a long time. He's an honest, upstanding man. A trustworthy man. And he's a doctor. A doctor would never…'

'No, he never would…' Ari Thór raised a cynical eyebrow.

'There's no way he could have done such a thing. It's just not possible, Ari Thór.'

Ugla didn't have to say another word. Ari Thór knew exactly what he had to do now.

40

'They're saying if this storm doesn't let up, there's going to be a blackout,' Ari Thór said, taking a seat across from Hersir in the cramped interview room at the police station. 'Hopefully the lights won't go out before we finish our little chat. This shouldn't take long.'

'I'm curious to know, Inspector, why it was so important for me to come here on a public holiday and in a raging blizzard.'

The doctor was clearly forcing himself to remain calm and courteous, as if telling himself this must be some sort of misunderstanding. But Ari Thór could sense the fear and apprehension beneath the man's mask of propriety.

His visit to Bjarki would have to wait a bit longer. A matter that was just as serious had come to light and could not be ignored.

'It's not particularly far away,' Ari Thór said.

'What?'

'The police station is a stone's throw from your front door.'

'Have you seen the weather outside? It's like the end of the world out there!'

'Welcome to winter in Siglufjörður. You'd better get used to it.'

Hersir bit his tongue and hung his head.

'I'd like to talk to you again about what Hávardur wrote on the wall of his room,' Ari Thór announced.

'I see … I thought all this was behind us, Inspector. He hasn't said a word about it, and it hasn't happened again.'

'Are you saying there's no need to take it seriously?'

Hersir hesitated. 'I don't think so. It's always hard to say with patients like him. You can't paint them all with the same brush, you know. The condition manifests itself in different ways in different people, and—'

'Can we not assume for a moment that Hávardur was telling the truth and that he did see something?' Ari Thór had heard enough of Hersir's waffling.

'I…'

'As I explained earlier, you are entitled to have a lawyer present for this interview.'

'No, I'm sure there's no need for that,' Hersir stammered. However, he didn't sound so sure of himself now.

'Do you want to know what I think? I think Hávardur witnessed a murder.'

Hersir didn't bat an eye.

'When I questioned him, he told me a certain Finnbogi had murdered a woman. He was adamant about it. But the thing is, I don't know anyone named Finnbogi, and neither does Ugla. And Hávardur himself wasn't forthcoming with any more details. It was only after I spoke with his son that I realised who Hávardur was talking about. I assume you know who Finnbogi is?'

'Yes,' Hersir sighed.

'Hávardur's former doctor,' Ari Thór stated.

Silence.

'My theory,' Ari Thór went on, 'is that Hávardur saw his doctor kill a woman. He just got the names mixed up. Hersir … Finnbogi … It's easily done, with the past and the present merging in his mind.'

Still the doctor said nothing.

'What did you do to her, Hersir? What did you do to the woman in the bed beside Hávardur's? Was the inheritance worth killing for? I've been led to believe that your finances were in an alarming state. Now, if I put two and two together...'

Hersir opened his mouth to speak, but nothing came out. Ari Thór waited for him to fill the silence.

'You have no idea how hard it was for us,' the doctor eventually replied. 'We're not exactly wallowing in cash. We put all our savings into buying the building, and the renovation work ended up costing a lot more than we had budgeted. Plus, the regulatory approvals took forever to come through, so we couldn't access government funding. We had to remortgage our house in Reykjavík as well as our place in Siglufjörður, just to make ends meet.'

'Let me guess: Rósa's aunt was already at death's door, so you figured there'd be no harm in helping her knock a bit louder,' Ari Thór surmised. 'You do know I can have her body exhumed to determine the cause of death, don't you?'

'She was already dead to the world. She had nothing to live for anymore. We thought she would pop her clogs at any minute. She had no one left besides the two of us. My wife and I.'

'Your wife was the sole heir, I gather.'

'Yes, she was. And she'd always taken such good care of her aunt over the years. We've always been there for her, so...'

'Tell me about the inheritance. Was it a significant sum of money?'

'Er, I don't recall the exact amount...'

'I can find that out. I've heard it was quite a generous figure.'

Hersir didn't say a word.

'More than enough to save you from bankruptcy, I gather,' Ari Thór added.

'The cash came in very handy,' was all Hersir said, after a brief silence. But his tone of voice suggested that he wished he had never seen the colour of that money – at least not at that precise moment.

'I had a little chat with Rósa,' Ari Thór continued. 'I think she's figured out what happened. Where is she at the moment, Hersir? I didn't see her when I came to bring you in to the station.'

'She must have gone out...'

'Out? In this weather? When it's getting dark and it's only a matter of time before the power goes out? Where would she have gone?'

'She ... she had made plans ... to see some people...'

He was lying, that much was obvious. Could Rósa have made a snap decision to pack her bags and walk out on him? Ari Thór could see the man was struggling to keep himself together. He might not realise it, but confessing to what he had done and facing the consequences of his actions would be a weight off his shoulders.

'Tell me what happened, Hersir,' Ari Thór said softly.

At that precise moment, the lights went out, plunging the cramped, windowless room into darkness.

41

Ari Thór froze and drew a sharp breath.

He had known a power cut was likely, but it still took him by surprise.

For a second, he was worried that Hersir would seize the opportunity to run. Time passed in slow motion as Ari Thór felt around in the dark for his phone, which he had left on the table. It was the only source of light within reach. But where the hell was it? His heart skipped a beat as he thought he heard Hersir moving. He hoped his imagination was playing tricks on him – he was making enough noise himself, scrabbling around on the table.

After what seemed like an eternity, his fingers found the phone. He activated the torch function and turned the beam towards where the doctor had been sitting.

Hersir hadn't moved. He was holding his head in his hands, as if he would rather stay in the dark. In the harsh, white beam cast by the torch, Ari Thór could see from the man's face that he was ready to concede defeat. He had been expecting him to put up more of a fight.

'It's all right, I'll go and fetch a lantern, or some candles,' Ari Thór said.

'Don't bother for my sake,' an indifferent Hersir replied.

Ari Thór waited in silence.

'She was on her last legs. And had been for a while. She was in a much weaker state than Hávardur is now. She can't have had more than a week or two left. Sometimes, I thought it was just a matter of days, but she seemed to keep hanging on by the skin of her teeth … She had nothing left to live for, can't you see?'

Ari Thór didn't say a word. He certainly didn't want the doctor to think he condoned what he had done.

'We were always a whisker away from pulling ourselves out of the spiral, but every time we thought we were getting somewhere, things got worse again. And we kept thinking about that money. It was just sitting there, within reach. And it wasn't benefiting anyone while she was still alive. We were about to lose our home – *both* our homes – as well as the care home, do you understand? Anyway, that night, I was sitting at her bedside, and I thought, *tonight's the night she's going to take her last breath*. I was sure Hávardur was asleep. I figured that even if he was awake, no one would take him seriously if he said anything. And then…'

Hersir's words faded into a long silence.

'You murdered her?' Ari Thór speculated.

The old-school tape recorder hissed and crackled away in the background. Ari Thór was glad it ran on batteries and had kept recording when the power went out. It was important to get Hersir's confession on tape.

'I wouldn't say I murdered her.'

'What, then?'

'I wasn't planning to do it. It wasn't premeditated. I just lost my patience, I suppose. I picked up a pillow and pressed it over her face for a few seconds. It didn't take very long. She wanted to be at peace. And I knew her, she would have been happy to know that her money was helping us out, and ultimately helping other people. Isn't that more like euthanasia than murder?'

'Follow me, Hersir. You're going to spend the night here. In a cell.'

'Here? You're going to leave me here … in the dark?'

His voice was shaking. Ari Thór suppressed the inkling of

empathy he felt rising within himself. He had to call Ögmundur now to tell him to come down to the station. Someone had to keep an eye on the doctor, and he wasn't going to do it himself.

Ari Thór could feel the adrenaline coursing through his veins.

Now it was time to pay Bjarki a visit. Ari Thór picked up his phone, thinking it best to call ahead, wary of spooking the man with an unexpected knock at the door during a blackout.

42

'Come in! I'm in my office,' Bjarki called from behind the door to his flat, which Ari Thór found ajar.

The door to the street had been left unlocked. Ari Thór had inched his way carefully up the stairs in the dark, fearful he might trip at any step. Now he pushed open the door to the flat and saw a faint glow coming from a small room down the hallway. Walking towards it, he couldn't help but feel like a moth being drawn to a flame.

He wasn't particularly comfortable to be venturing alone, in the dark, into the home of a man against whom he was about to level some serious allegations. He wouldn't have been averse to the idea of Ögmundur joining him on this house call.

He walked past the pitch-dark living room and peered into the doorway of the office, to find Bjarki sitting at his desk with a number of tall candles perched on old-fashioned candlesticks in front of him. Ari Thór couldn't help but feel like he had stepped a century back in time.

As he entered the doorway, the man looked up with eyes like thunder clouds. Ari Thór wasn't sure if it was fear or concern he could read on his face. It was hard to tell which of them was the most on edge.

'I was trying to read by candlelight. I can't say I'm having much success,' Bjarki said, to break the ice.

'I can imagine,' Ari replied, still standing in the doorway.

He hoped the historian would invite him to sit down in the living room, but he wasn't holding his breath. Instead, the man seemed content to sit at his desk and look expectantly at his visitor.

Ari Thór knew very well how he wanted to approach this conversation. He had been planning to observe Bjarki's reactions closely. But the darkened room would complicate that somewhat.

'We've found her phone,' he announced, after an intentionally uncomfortable pause.

Silence.

'Whose phone?'

'Unnur's.'

'I wouldn't have known it was missing,' Bjarki replied.

'I'm talking about her second phone. The one she kept hidden,' Ari Thór said coldly. 'The one you tried to find when you broke into Salvör's house.'

Bjarki gave a theatrical laugh. 'I broke into her house? Wherever did you get that ridiculous idea?'

'It happened the very night you returned to Siglufjörður – somewhat earlier than planned, I might add.'

'Like I told you, I changed my plans,' Bjarki snapped. 'Wouldn't you have done the same thing? Someone threw herself off the balcony above my flat. Obviously, I was quite concerned.'

'You knew what was on that phone. And you wanted to make sure we didn't get our hands on it.'

Bjarki's calm appearance splintered. 'What was on there? Go on then, spit it out!'

'Let's just say there were some eye-opening messages between the two of you...'

'Between me and her?' He whistled. Then, after a moment's silence, said, 'I can show you my phone, if you like. There's not a single message on there from Unnur. I barely knew the girl. You can't just turn up at my front door throwing around those kinds of accusations...'

'I haven't accused you of anything, Bjarki,' Ari Thór replied calmly.

The historian was more than flustered now. 'What? I … No, well, not directly. But you know what I mean…'

'I just wanted to see your reaction, Bjarki. I gather that Unnur wasn't the only schoolgirl you took a shine to.'

'What?'

'You neglected to tell me that you had been her teacher.'

'For heaven's sake, you can't expect me to remember the names of all my students! It was only a replacement position. I was there just a month or two, at the most.'

'Are you saying there were others? Besides Unnur?'

Bjarki sprang up from his chair and boomed: 'I was in Reykjavík when she threw herself off the balcony! You know that very well. Your colleague even made a bunch of phone calls to check. I didn't do anything. I didn't do a thing to her.'

'No one's saying that you pushed her off that balcony, Bjarki.' *Not physically*, he wanted to add. 'She rang the bell downstairs at Jóhann and Jónína's, they buzzed her into the building, she walked up to the attic, and she jumped. It's a tragedy.'

Ari Thór marked a pause.

'She was only nineteen years old.'

'I know. And I don't see what you're doing here, if you've reached a verdict of suicide.'

'Would you like me to read out some of the messages you exchanged?'

'I never sent her any messages. Like I said, all you have to do is check my phone.'

'Of course, I'm not going to find anything on there. You used a different phone. You have your ways and means. Chances are, if we turn your flat upside down we'll find another phone. Or perhaps you've got rid of it already?'

'I haven't done anything!' Bjarki cried.

'You know what? I think I will read some of those messages to you. I'll start with the juiciest of them all. The ones where you threaten to post naked photos of her online if she breaks up with you…'

'I don't know what you're talking about,' Bjarki protested loudly, but his words were far from convincing. 'And I don't want to hear any more about it. It's none of my business. And then he had the gall to add, 'Surely she has a right to privacy…'

'Do you think it's normal for someone to receive those kinds of threats? It's illegal. You do realise that, don't you?'

'What? This is ridiculous. Whatever happened to freedom of expression?' Bjarki protested. The words seemed to stick in his mouth.

'Do you think it's normal to have a relationship with a nineteen-year-old schoolgirl, Bjarki?' Ari Thór pressed.

He didn't reply straight away.

'You know nothing about my private life, and it's none of your damn business anyway. There's nothing illegal about having a younger girlfriend. It's not against the law.'

'So, you're admitting you've had a younger girlfriend? A nineteen-year-old one? And perhaps not just one?'

'No, no, I never said that…'

Bjarki retreated to the safety of his office chair.

'You know we have ways of finding things out, Bjarki. We can easily trace where a prepaid mobile SIM card came from, and we can review the CCTV from the shop where it was purchased. And that's just the tip of the iceberg. By the way, I'd like you to know that another young woman is willing to go on the record about your relationship, if need be. But I haven't finished talking about that second phone of Unnur's yet. We can trace where that phone has been and compare it to yours. We've already sent her smartphone – the one she didn't keep hidden – to Reykjavík for analysis. We can easily overlap the data from that phone with her secret phone to track her movements. And from there, it'll be a breeze to figure out when and where the two of you were together.'

'Listen, it wasn't my fault,' Bjarki blurted. 'I'm not responsible for her killing herself. I didn't push her.'

'No one actually pushed her, Bjarki. But there is such a thing as provocation – driving someone to their death indirectly.'

'No there isn't!' Bjarki yelled, but he was fast running out of steam. 'You're not going to pin this on me. There's no such thing as indirect murder. You can't haul someone in front of a judge for that.'

His voice faltered, as if he was trying to convince himself that was true.

'That's quite right,' Ari Thór simply replied.

'What?' Bjarki leaned forward with a sigh.

'I can't charge you with murder, but I can order you to report to the police station tomorrow so I can take a statement concerning these threats. I also have a duty to alert the high school to the situation. I doubt they'll be keen to call on your services again.'

'You can't … you won't…' Realising resistance was futile, he bit his tongue.

'But above all else, you'll have to learn to live with the death of a teenage girl on your conscience. I wouldn't want to be in your shoes.'

Bjarki looked aghast.

'I think that will be all for now,' Ari Thór concluded.

'You can't do this,' the historian hissed under his breath.

'Do what?'

'Threaten me like that. I'll never be able to live here again. I'll have to move away and finish my book somewhere else.'

Ari Thór had to stifle a smile. Clearly, Bjarki hadn't grasped the fact that everything was about to change, and his chances of keeping his funding from the town council would be close to non-existent when the whole sordid affair came to light.

He carried on, more for his own benefit than Ari Thór's. 'I'll go to Siglunes. I'll just leave earlier than I planned. At least no one there will be on my back.'

43

Ari Thór's pulse quickened, but he tried not to let it show. 'Siglunes? I was there this weekend,' he said, reflexively.

Bjarki glared at him. 'No—'

'Yes, I was. I went by boat with Reverend Eggert. I'd never been there before. I imagine you know the father and son who live out there?'

'You've misunderstood,' Bjarki replied. 'I'm not talking about the place at the end of the fjord. I'm talking about Siglunes in Canada, where many of the Icelanders who emigrated to North America settled.'

'What?'

'Siglunes is an old village on the shore of Lake Manitoba. Well, technically it's not called that anymore. They changed the name recently. I'm renting a cabin there, down by the water. When the Icelandic immigrants arrived over there, they named the places they settled in after familiar places back home.'

But Ari Thór didn't hear his last few words. The image of what Unnur had written in her planner was before his eyes, and he now realised its significance.

Siglunes. She had been planning to join him over there. She had been planning to follow the man she thought she was in love with, all the way to Canada; and then her life shattered into pieces.

'Why couldn't you just leave her in peace?' he suddenly interrupted.

'What?'

'Why couldn't you just swallow your pride and leave her to get on with her life? She'd still be alive today…'

Bjarki showed no signs of remorse.

'What you did was shameful – threatening to post intimate photos online of a young woman who had her whole life to look forward to. What the hell were you thinking?'

Ari Thór bit his tongue. He knew he shouldn't let his anger at the man get the better of him, but he couldn't help raising his voice. No matter what Bjarki claimed, the responsibility for Unnur's death should weigh on his shoulders.

'Were you planning to take her with you to Canada? Is that what she thought?' He took a step towards the historian, who recoiled in his chair as if he thought Ari Thór was going to lash out at him. Obviously, Ari Thór did not intend to cross that line; however, by moving closer he could better observe the man's reactions.

'I have another question for you,' he continued, taking another step towards the man, who now seemed to be cowering in his chair. 'Did you really intend to post those photos online? I doubt it. She would have ended up turning it against you. She would have reported you. So she essentially died for nothing. Desperate and terrified … and all because of you.'

He turned on his heels and strode to the door, with an empty, sickened feeling in the pit of his stomach. Stopping in the doorway, he cast a glance over his shoulder. Bjarki hadn't moved a muscle; he was still sitting at his desk in the flickering candlelight, with a dejected look on his face. Perhaps it was just Ari Thór's imagination, but it seemed the candles weren't burning as brightly as before.

44

That evening, Ari Thór was lying naked by Ugla's side when his phone rang.

The power still hadn't come back on. As if the lights going out wasn't bad enough, the heating wasn't working either. Ari Thór had spent most of the day at the station with Ögmundur, and for much of that time he had been speaking to the mayor and the local search-and-rescue coordinators on the phone. During a prolonged power cut, it was customary for the search-and-rescue teams to knock on every door to distribute candles and battery-powered torches to residents. Hersir was still in custody at the station, and Bjarki was a free man, so to speak.

At eight o'clock, Ari Thór had knocked at Ugla's door, as he had promised, determined not to make a faux pas this time.

One thing had led to another, but he had left his phone on the bedside table, just in case. Not that he wanted to be disturbed – it was past ten o'clock already and he had no intention of getting out of bed before daybreak – but work was important to him, and the habit of keeping his phone close by was ingrained.

He could have said that the evening had soon taken an unexpected turn, but deep down he had to admit it was exactly what he had been hoping for. And now he had every intention of spending all night by Ugla's side.

For some reason, Ari Thór found himself thinking about the first time he had met Kristín, at a party for a mutual friend's birthday. They had both been so young. Ari Thór hadn't known what he wanted. He was still just a student – not to mention an orphan – trying to find his way. She was always much more organised, determined and driven than him, but something had clicked between them and they had made it work. And then, some seven years later, Ari Thór had met Ugla. Now that he thought about it, the spark with her had immediately felt more powerful than the love he had for Kristín. The chemistry between him and Ugla had been there right from the beginning. Everything just seemed so easy and effortless.

And now, years later, the time seemed right for them to give things another go. The future was promising.

When the phone rang, Ugla rolled over and placed a hand on his shoulder.

'Don't answer it … just ignore it,' she whispered with a seductive smile.

He hesitated.

'It's this storm, you know…' he apologised. 'I have to…'

He hadn't had a chance to tell her they had taken Hersir into custody. That could wait until the morning.

'Don't worry, I'm only joking. Go on, answer it,' she urged.

Ugla was always so relaxed and seemed to take things in her stride. She never made a fuss.

Ari Thór sat up in bed and reached for his phone. The caller display told him it was Salvör, Unnur's mother. He decided to ignore the call, thinking she would hang up, but the phone kept ringing. He turned to Ugla, who simply smiled and shrugged.

'Hello, this is Inspector Ari Thór Arason,' he replied, with the same formal tone he used when he was on duty.

'I'm sorry to bother you so late,' Salvör said. 'But I really need to talk to you. There's something I have to tell you.'

'Can't it wait until tomorrow? I'll be happy to see you at the station in the morning. I'm busy right now…'

'I'm afraid it's very urgent.'

'I suppose I can spare a few minutes, if you're able to tell me over the phone,' he conceded.

But Salvör wasn't going to back down. 'Please, can you come to the house? I need to tell you face to face. It won't take long, I promise.'

Ari Thór swore under his breath and turned to Ugla.

'Hang on a second, Salvör.'

He muted the microphone on his handset.

'It's Unnur's mother, and it sounds urgent. Do you mind if I step out for half an hour?'

His head was spinning. Could there still be more to uncover about the young woman's death?

'Not at all, Ari Thór,' Ugla replied. 'The poor woman's lost her daughter, so if speaking to you for a while helps her, that's all right with me. I'm not getting out of bed. I'll be waiting when you get back,' she added, with a wicked glint in her eye.

'All right,' he sighed. 'I'll be quick.'

He unmuted his phone.

'I can come over right now, Salvör. Does that work for you?'

'Oh, yes. Thank you,' she replied.

'I only have about half an hour, though,' he warned her.

'That'll be long enough.'

'I'm on my way.'

He hung up, pulled some clothes on and leaned down to kiss Ugla.

'Don't be too long, now. A woman can't wait forever…'

'I promise.'

It filled him with an unpleasant feeling to hear himself say those words. How many promises in his life had he made – and broken without meaning to? He suddenly thought about his father and all the promises and responsibilities he had abandoned when he disappeared into thin air overnight.

'I won't be long, I promise,' he repeated, in spite of himself.

45

As the heavy snowflakes swirled around him and the frigid north wind whipped at his face, Ari Thór started to doubt that he had actually brought this investigation to the right conclusion. Had he somehow made a mistake? Could he have been led towards the wrong deduction? What could Salvör possibly have to say that was so urgent and couldn't wait until the morning? Everything had happened so quickly, he had to remind himself that it had only been four days since Unnur's body was found.

What did Salvör know? Had she somehow…?

There was no way she could have had a hand in her daughter's death, was there? No, of course not, he thought. That would be completely absurd.

He let his mind wander as he trudged through the snowdrifts.

Could she have been hiding something from him? If so, why come clean now? Perhaps a new clue, a new piece of evidence, had come to light.

He couldn't stand the thought that he might not have slotted a piece of the puzzle into the right place. What if he had overlooked an important detail?

As he walked up to the house, he felt a growing sense of unease, as if a threat was lurking behind the front door. For a second, he considered calling Ögmundur for backup, but thought better of it. He wasn't in danger. There was nothing to be afraid of.

The raging storm and the blackout had plunged the house into darkness, like everywhere else in the area. Ari Thór shivered, but dismissed the feeling, attributing it solely to the cold.

The sound of the doorbell echoed inside the house, and Salvör opened the door in a flash. Her face was ravaged by anguish.

'Come in.' She led him into the living room, where a single candle flickered on the coffee table.

'Thank you. I'm afraid I don't have a lot of time,' he said, as politely as he could muster.

'Let's sit down, shall we ... Yes, let's make ourselves comfortable,' Salvör mumbled, almost to herself, as if she hadn't heard a word he'd just said.

Ari Thór sat across from her, on the other side of the coffee table. In the candle's faint light, she looked deathly pale. She remained desperately silent, as if she didn't know where to begin.

46

'Once again, you have all my sympathies, Salvör. I can only imagine what you must be going through,' Ari Thór ventured, to break the silence.

He let the words hang in the air for a moment, thinking they might be grounding for her. However, his effort proved fruitless. Salvör remained consumed by her silence, staring at the floor, trembling with anxiety.

Ari Thór tried to be patient, mentally counting every passing second, wondering how much time he should give her. Maybe she just needed someone to talk to. If so, Ari Thór wasn't sure he was the right person. Surely Reverend Eggert would be better placed to help her.

His thoughts turned to Ugla, alone at home. He was pleasantly surprised to realise he was missing her already.

'I didn't know if I should call you,' Salvör suddenly blurted out, making Ari Thór jump. 'I mulled it over for a while. But I told myself it would be a bad idea to say anything.'

Ari Thór sat up and listened. So she had been keeping a secret. What – or who – had she been protecting?

'It's never too late to tell the truth,' he said, watching for her reaction.

She seemed completely detached, as if she was coming to grips with a terrible shock. Again, Ari Thór sensed that his words weren't getting through to her. She was hiding beneath a thick, impenetrable shell.

'She didn't have to die. I've been telling myself that over and over since the last time I saw you, Ari Thór. It all seems so pointless. She never caused any trouble, never strayed from the straight and narrow. She had a bright future ahead of her, and such high ambitions. If I close my eyes, I can still hear her voice … I can hear her telling me what she wants to do after university. I've barely slept. If I do manage to drift away, she comes to me in my dreams, and…'

She released a long sigh.

'And I know how it happened. Believe me, I know how it happened…'

And then, for the first time since Ari Thór had set foot in the door, she looked into his eyes.

47

'Are you suggesting she wasn't alone on the balcony?' Ari Thór asked.

'Not alone?' Salvör exclaimed, not bothering to hide her surprise. 'What are you getting at? Of course she was alone up there. She jumped; you know that.'

'It sounded like you might have some new information,' Ari Thór explained.

'You don't get it, do you? That sleazy bastard wasn't with her that night. He was in Reykjavík, he's made that clear enough. But he might as well have been up there on that balcony, because we all know he pushed her to it.'

Ari Thór nodded. 'I expect he'll be charged with making those threats. I'm going to take a formal statement from him tomorrow. I suspect he'll be in a hurry to leave town, so you won't have to worry about running into him.'

Salvör's eyes glazed over. 'I had to talk to him. He came here earlier.'

Ari Thór held his breath, wondering where this was going. 'You asked him into your house?' he asked.

'I wanted to hear what he had to say for himself. I wanted to show him Unnur's room. So he could see what he'd stolen from me…'

'Did he tell you anything you didn't already know?'

Salvör looked at him as if she didn't understand the question.

'Did he tell me anything? Like what?' she fumed. 'There's nothing more to say. One way or another, he pushed my daughter off that balcony. He killed her with those shameful threats of his. What kind of man does something like that, Ari Thór? My Unnur was still a child.'

It seemed clear to Ari Thór that Salvör had simply asked him over because she was distraught and needed someone to talk to. It was perfectly understandable. She was a mother grieving the death of her daughter, and she was struggling to make sense of what had happened. She was alone and powerless, torn apart by a desperation to which there was no end. Alone in the darkness, trapped in a maelstrom of memories.

Ari Thór couldn't fathom the depth of suffering she must be going through. Perhaps she had considered suicide herself. Perhaps her phone call to Ari Thór was a call for help – one last attempt to cling on to life. He made a mental note to keep an eye on her and make sure she came to no harm of her own doing.

But Ari Thór doubted he would be able to give her the help she needed. As far as he could see, Salvör had lost touch with reality.

'I can only imagine how hard this must be for you,' was all he said.

Salvör hung her head between her knees. Ari Thór was expecting her to start crying, but all he could hear was a deafening silence.

48

She drew herself straight and looked him right in the eye. The expression on her face was so cold, it gave him the shivers.

'You have no idea. Times like this, all we can do is try to cope. Each in our own way.'

'Would you like me to call Reverend Eggert?' Ari Thór offered. 'Perhaps you'd like to talk to him and see if he has any advice to share with you…'

'Eggert?' she smirked. 'No, I don't think so. He can't do anything for me. He's nice enough, but talking to him would be a waste of time.'

'Are you sure?'

'I'm certain.'

'Are you really sure you don't want me to call someone for you, Salvör? It's not good for you to be alone.'

'There's no point. There's just no point…' she murmured, her voice fading to a haunting whisper.

'It's no trouble at all,' Ari Thór assured her. 'There's no need to feel bad about it.'

He was starting to lose patience. He suspected that no matter how much he tried to help Salvör find some support, she would never accept the offers of a shoulder to lean on.

'Did it help to get things off your chest at least, when you spoke to Bjarki? Was it a relief?' he asked, after a brief silence.

She looked away, pondering the question. 'A relief? I don't know that it was, Ari Thór. I don't think so.'

She heaved a long sigh.

'Did he tell you anything you didn't know, Salvör? Anything you'd like us to look into more closely?'

She nodded. 'Yes … he said he was sorry for what happened. He kept saying it, over and over again…'

'That was the least he could do,' Ari Thór replied, simply to add punctuation to her words.

Salvör carried on, oblivious. 'But he didn't apologise for his relationship with my daughter. He told me he loved her, but…' She swallowed a lump in her throat. 'But how could he love her, Ari Thór? It was wrong. She was a teenage girl. And he was a grown man. He was her *teacher*. I can't wrap my head around it.'

There was nothing Ari Thór could say. He was in charge of the investigation, but he was powerless to change anything. He was just a spectator watching a twisted tragedy unravel before his eyes. He didn't have what it would take to provide this poor woman with the support she so desperately needed. Things might have been different, though, if he had finished his theology studies before joining the police.

But Salvör had more to say. 'He refused to take responsibility.'

'How so?'

'For Unnur's death. He kept saying he was sorry, again and again, for what happened, but when I told him he was the one to blame – that he had driven her to her death – he shrugged it off. There must have been other factors at play – anxiety, depression, or something, that's what he said. He said it wasn't his fault that she did what she did. He said it wasn't fair to make him carry her death on his conscience for the rest of his life…'

'They're only words, Salvör. Try not to let him get to you. You know as well as I do where the burden of responsibility lies.'

Staring vacantly across the room, she continued. 'Is it *fair* that I have to live with what he did? That I have to live on my own in this great big house now he's snatched her away from me? Is that fair, Ari Thór?'

'No, it isn't.'

He stood up.

'I have to go now, Salvör. I'll check in with you tomorrow, all right?'

She followed his lead, picking up the candlestick as she rose from her chair. Then she looked him straight in the eye with grim determination.

'No, you can't leave. Not yet.'

She took a step towards him, sending a shiver down his spine.

49

She was standing close, far too close to him, encroaching on his personal space. It forced him to take a few steps back, glancing over his shoulder to avoid bumping into the furniture.

'I really do have to go now,' he repeated, more firmly this time. 'Unless there's something you've forgotten to tell me?' he added, sensing she still had something important to say.

'Yes.'

He froze and held her gaze.

'Something important?'

He had a sickening feeling that something wasn't right.

'Follow me,' Salvör said slowly and deliberately, leading him into the hallway and up the stairs towards her daughter's room, their only source of light the flickering candle she held in her hand.

'What did you want to tell me, Salvör?' Ari Thór pressed.

She stopped on the landing at the top of the stairs. 'I have to show you something.'

Continuing on her way, she stopped again outside Unnur's room. Then she handed the candlestick to Ari Thór and pushed the door open.

Before Ari Thór had a chance to peer into the darkened room, she cast a glance over her shoulder at him and whispered: 'Forgive me.'

He wasn't sure if her words were meant for him or for someone else, perhaps her late daughter, or a god he himself no longer believed in.

'Forgive you for what?' he asked, as he stepped into the room.

And then he saw, in the faint, flickering candlelight, a scene that made him recoil in horror.

'No … what the…?'

He was lost for words. Stepping carefully into the room for a closer look, it crossed his mind for a second that he might be in danger himself. No, that was unlikely, he quickly told himself. Still, he looked over his shoulder to make sure Salvör was a good distance away. Leaning against the door frame, she looked like a broken woman.

Bjarki's body was lying on the floor in a pool of blood. No signs of life were apparent. Instinctively keeping an eye trained on Salvör, who hadn't moved, Ari Thór crouched down to check for a pulse – and failed to detect one.

He reached for his phone and called Ögmundur to explain the situation.

Figuring time was of the essence, the young rookie insisted there was no harm in leaving Hersir alone in his cell at the station for a while. While he was en route he would radio for an ambulance and doctor to attend the scene. Even though there was clearly nothing more that could be done for Bjarki.

Once Ari Thór had hung up, he turned to Salvör and gave her a questioning look. Convinced that she wasn't a danger to him, he decided to listen patiently to what she had to say.

'I don't know … I don't know what possessed me…' she sobbed.

Ari Thór had felt so much empathy for her. In the few days since her daughter's death, he had seen how deeply grief and loneliness had dug their claws into her. She was the victim who would have to live with the consequences of this terrible tragedy. But the image in his mind of the grieving mother had just been torn to shreds. His empathy for her had slipped away as swiftly as the fleeting winter sun. Now – and he couldn't be sure if he was just imagining it – the only thing he could see in her was a merciless glint in her eye.

'You have to believe me, Ari Thór, I didn't mean the man any harm. I just wanted him to admit what he'd done and assume the consequences. I wanted him to show me he regretted his actions. None of that would have brought her back, I know, but it was important for me to hear him own up to it. You have to understand, I was suffering so terribly … It was tearing me apart.'

Ari Thór didn't doubt that for a second.

'But he just shrugged it off and refused to admit responsibility. He was burying his head in the sand. So I suggested we go up to her room. *Her childhood room.* I wanted to show him that my daughter was still a child. But then something happened that I wasn't expecting.'

She paused and drew a sharp breath.

'Bjarki knew where he was going. He barged past me and went straight to her door and pushed it wide open. That was when I realised he'd been in here before. That was when I saw red.'

50

Needless to say, it was late when Ari Thór knocked at Ugla's door for the second time that night.

Salvör had readily confessed to her crime: she had flown into a blind rage and grabbed the first object within reach – a heavy crystal vase Unnur had been given for her first communion – before lunging at the man. A single blow would likely have sufficed, but she had been so hell-bent on delivering her own form of justice that she had kept on hitting him, again and again, until there could be no doubt.

Part of her seemed to regret what she had done. A small part of her.

On reflection, perhaps she felt she had done what she had to do – after all, she had nothing left to lose. For now, she had been taken into custody at the station to spend the night in a cramped cell next to Hersir's. Ögmundur was there to keep an eye on them both.

It took Ugla a while to answer the door. He had obviously woken her up. In spite of her yawning and eye-rubbing, she gave him a warm smile.

'You were a bit longer than I expected. I tried to keep my eyes open, but they kept closing by themselves. Before I knew it, I was out like a light.'

Ari Thór had texted her a few times to let her know he had been held up, but hadn't explained why.

'I'm sorry,' he said, and meant it.

'Is everything all right? I was worried about you.'

'I'm all right, it's just…'

He didn't quite know how to go about explaining the

chilling chain of events that evening. To be honest, he didn't feel like talking about it. Not right now, anyway.

Ugla leaned forward and kissed him.

'Shhh, you can tell me all about it in the morning. Come with me,' she whispered in his ear.

He followed her inside and double-checked that the door had locked behind him. It was freezing inside her flat, he realised with a shiver as he took off his parka. Of course; the power was still out.

'The radiators went cold a while ago,' she said, as if she had read his mind. 'Let's find a way to keep each other warm under the duvet, shall we?' she added with a twinkle in her eye.

Ari Thór smiled, and a rush of happiness surged through him. Maybe this was what it felt like to come home, he thought.

ACKNOWLEDGEMENTS

Dear Readers,

I hope you have enjoyed meeting Ari Thór again. I started writing about him over ten years ago and then took a break for a few years, but the story that features in *Winterkill* was always at the back of my mind, and I knew I had to write it. The fantastic support from readers was also so encouraging.

Ari Thór first found his way to English-speaking readers in 2014, following a football match in Scotland, where I played on the same team as publisher Karen Sullivan. Upon encouragement from author and translator Quentin Bates, she decided to take a chance on an Icelandic author for her new publishing house, Orenda Books. That decision, and the amazing enthusiasm of both Karen and Quentin, opened up a whole new world of readers for the Dark Iceland series, for which I am incredibly grateful. The people of Siglufjörður have also been so generous, tolerating the level of crime that takes place in my books in this beautiful seaside village. My parents, Jónas Ragnarsson and Katrín Guðjónsdóttir, have also helped bring Ari Thór to readers, reviewing proofs of the novels in Icelandic. I am also very grateful for the level of support from so many friends in the international crime-fiction community, even before my books were translated into English, crime-fiction experts such as Barry Forshaw, John Curran and Bob Cornwell, and fellow authors such as Yrsa Sigurðardóttir, Ian Rankin, Ann Cleeves, Lee Child, Anthony Horowitz, Peter James, William Ryan and Craig Robertson. My friend Hulda Maria Stefansdóttir, a prosecutor in Iceland, has been Ari Thór's advisor in relation to the technical side of police work throughout the series. Also, I'm very grateful to my amazing agents, David Headley from DHH Literary Agency and Monica Gram from Copenhagen Literary Agency, who have sent Ari Thór on a wonderful trip around the world, and Emily Hayward-Whitlock at The Artists Partnership, who is very committed to bringing Ari Thor to the screen as soon as possible. Warm thanks also to the excellent translators who transformed *Winterkill* into French and English editions, Jean-Christophe Salaün and David Warriner. And as always, thanks to my wife and daughters, María, Kira and Natalía, for their endless support and understanding.

If you want to keep in touch with Ari, his email address is arithorarason@gmail.com.